LiT
Part II – Falling Lite
2024 Edition

Maxwell F. Hurley

LiT
Part II – Falling Lite
2024 Edition

FICTION4ALL

DEDICATION

This book is dedicated to
the victims and survivors of domestic violence
"Power and Bravery is within you."

Thank you to my beta readers:
Cami Espiritu
Ashley Jarvenpaa

Part II – Falling Lite

Introduction

Salamor hovered over a sleeping homeless man in the street. He never understood how the primates never took care of each other if they were supposed to be full of love for their God. He could smell the odor of urine-soaked clothes. Even though he was a Demon Myst, the smell made him sick. He fully understood why Vandor was dedicated to the Dark to regain control of the primates. They didn't know how to handle themselves. The Dark would rule over them, keep them in line, make them work with a purpose and then continue to understand that power once their mortal life was distinguished.

Salamor was scouting looking for just the right person for Vandor. He had some time before he needed someone with the right heart, but he liked to keep one in mind just in case. They seemed to be harder and harder to come by. Salamor continued to go person to person to find for consumption. He sniffed a primate whore who was working on a male who was obviously married. Salamor thought he would have some fun with her so he whispered in her ear for a moment until she had a sense of hopelessness he could pounce on, but she quickly regained her focus to continue her work. Salamor got frustrated but came across a couple who were fighting in their apartment. He floated through the window to sense the feel of despair. It was not coming from the adult primates, but someone else.

This feeling was in no doubt something he could pass the time with.

He floated into the room in the shadows where he saw a young teenage girl crying into her pillow while listening to music. She was trying to drown out the yelling from the older primates. He floated next to her bed and studied her face. He never really studied the features of a primate up close before. He really didn't see what the big deal was. He guessed she was attractive by primate standards but that was no matter. He leaned close to her ear, "do it." The girl continued to cry. He changed the approach and floated to her other ear, "no one will miss you." The girl got out of bed. She wiped the tears from her face as she looked at old pictures of her family. "You'd be better off," he continued hovering over her. The girl opened the drawer to her desk where there was a bottle of pills next to a Bible. Salamor cringed at the thought of her opening that book. But she grabbed the pills instead, she read them and then she looked to the door where she heard her parents fighting. "Show them," Salamor whispered to her.

The young, teenage girl opened the bottle. She took all the pills, washing them down with a hidden bottle of alcohol she had hid in her closet. There was no turning back now. Salamor took advantage of the situation, "The window." The little girl stumbled to the window and pushed out the screen. Salamor looked down at the distance; he knew the fall would end this young girl's life. "One step," he said. The little girl got onto the ledge of the window. Salamor floated outside of the window where he motioned for her to come to him as his demon's eyes flashed. "Do it." The little girl took one last drink from her bottle as she stepped forward. She fell to the ground, breaking her mortal body. Salamor was pleased with his accomplishment. He soared down to the girl lying on the pavement below. The open eyes of the lifeless body just stared at him as he studied her. A feeling of accomplishment consummated over himself.

Then a light caught Salamor's attention as a skinny girl with a pale face came running up to the girl with fists glowing blue. Accompanied her was a massive creature on four legs running up to him. He flew back to the wall to watch from shadows where he was most comfortable. He watched as the Lite Sentry examined the body. He could see her open her communication device as she was calling, asking someone for help.

Salamor heard the scream of a woman coming from up above. He looked to see a woman screaming for her child as the father tried holding her back. Salamor snickered. He went to gaze upon the lifeless body in front but he was met with the Lite Sentry face to face.

"Why?" She asked him.

Salamor watched as her colossal companion joined her side growling. He just stared back at her. "Why not?" he questioned back. "How does it feel to know you are failing?" Her eyes flashed as she swung at Salamor. Her fists went through him like a land machine through fog. "You are a fool as much as you are a failure. You are worthless. No one is to love you."

She regained her bearings. "You need to leave, or I will find a way to kill you." She straightened up her outfit. The purple creature growled at Salamor and then turned to join his master's side.

Salamor floated off into the darkness of the alley as he hollered back at her, "No one, Sentry."

Chapter 1

Anne had managed to shut off her alarm before it was set to wake her up. She didn't want to wake Kale up from his sleep. He was getting little as of late. He was tossing and turning a lot lately these past couple of months. The size of the dorm beds was not conducive for two people, so the movement was really noticeable. It didn't really matter though, because she enjoyed lying next to him. Anne nestled closer to him as he squeezed his arm around her stomach. She could not help but to smile. Anne peeked over at his roommate who was sleeping soundly in the bed on the other side of the room. Kameron was a nice guy, but she didn't know too much about him as he pretty much kept to himself. She managed to slowly move Kale's arm from around her as she picked up her shoes. She grabbed her keys for the car, trying not to make any sounds. It was a half hour drive before she got home, and she had to get ready for her advanced class on religious history.

She leaned over and kissed Kale on the forehead, "I gotta go."

Kale murmured, "Do you have to? What time is it?"

"5:30 in the morning. I have my early class today," Anne answered. "I will call you when I get done."

Kale winced as he rolled over. He opened his eyes and smiled. He ran his fingers through her wavy brown hair. "Dinner tonight?" He playfully pushed on the center of her glasses.

She kissed his hands, "I will pick you up at five." She smiled at him as he returned in kind.

"Can't wait." He tried to get up to kiss Anne, but she pushed him down.

"No, no, you stay down," Anne bent over to kiss him instead. The two kissed as she had a hard time saying good-bye. She giggled as he tried to keep her close to him, "I really need to go."

***

Mole smiled at Anne because she was cute as a button as she tried not to disturb his roommate with her leaving. He still got a tingling rush as she blew him a kiss goodbye, giggling. He knew she had to go to class. It still didn't make watching her leave any easier. She quietly shut the door and he laid in bed debating if he would start trying to get up. He had the energy; the problem was every morning it was getting more and more painful for him to get out of bed. His back was completely stiff, and it hurt him to walk until his back got warmed up a bit. He heard his roommate start to roll over as he turned off his alarm. Mole liked Kameron as far as he knew of him. He just did his thing. He went to the gym, class, gym, studying, and bed, that's all he knew of him. That, and the fact he was from a small town north of New York. Kameron got up and gave a nod as he got into his bathrobe and headed to the community bathroom.

Mole tried to get up, but a sharp pain shot from his back. He continued to lie in bed waiting for the pain to subside before he attempted to get out again. He rolled over to his side so he could swing his legs onto the floor. He took a moment for more pain to leave. Once the sensation dissipated, he limped over to his desk where he grabbed some pain medication. He took the dosage prescribed as he stretched his back out. It took a bit for him to warm up his back before he could walk normally, but he really needed to be careful not to overdo it throughout the day.

He put on his bathrobe which Anne had put over his chair at his desk. She must have used it when she took a shower last night as Mole was sleeping. He really appreciated the sacrifices she was making to keep their relationship going. At least once during the week she would spend the night over in his dorm room and meet up four to five times a week for dinner, studying together, or just to hang out.

The door opened and Kameron came in as Mole walked to the bathroom. The sound of a door opening down the hall caught Mole's attention. A blonde girl who was obviously wearing the same clothes she wore last night was sneaking out of the room. She gave him a quick embarrassed smile as she walked barefoot down the hallway, holding her high heels. Mole smiled in return and continued to get ready for his day.

***

Alex walked into her shared apartment with Komptin at her side. She was sure to be quiet because she didn't know if Anne and Brenda were sleeping or not. Brenda was a roommate who had answered an ad Anne placed in the student lounge at her school. Alex didn't really care for her too much; she was nice but not too smart. Brenda reminded Alex of a typical California Valley Girl. She talked like a ditz and she looked down at people she didn't think were up to her standard.

Anne offered the master bedroom of the house to Alex so she would have enough room for Komptin. Alex used her skills to quietly sneak past the two other rooms. The door squeaked when Alex opened it. Komptin jumped on the bed and got comfortable. Alex thought it was ironic because her side effect from being a Lite Sentry was in full swing. She hadn't slept for two years, but her furry companion over there could sleep at a drop of a hat. She actually missed the feeling of being tired and falling asleep in a nice, warm bed. The only time Alex got into the bed was to read or if she hooked up with someone for the night. Other than that, Komptin had it made, and he was not shy about taking advantage of it.

Komptin went immediately to bed and started to snore. Alex got undressed and put her bathrobe on to get ready to jump in the shower. She sat down at the foot of the bed so Komptin could put his head on her lap. She scratched her faithful companion behind the ears. He slowly opened his eyes into a sad stare. Alex got up to see what he was looking at so intently through the window. The fall months kept the mornings dark and the stars out later. Alex gazed upon the purple star shining bright for only her and Komptin to see. "I miss him too," Alex said. She sat back down on the bench at the foot of the bed and hugged her dog. "I hope I am doing him proud." Komptin licked Alex on the cheek. Alex laughed. "Gross." She ruffled him up a bit and Komptin playfully tried to bite her hands. "I gotta get ready for class." She got up to take a shower. She got undressed and stared at herself in the mirror. She looked at the scar on the side of her neck. An infiltrator had possessed Sara's dad, making him into a demon. Alex hunted him down and during their fight he dug his claw into her neck. Then she looked over some of the other scars. Most of them were faint but one or two were quite noticeable. She wondered how anybody would accept her as a Sentry.

***

Anne got out of her car and buttoned up her coat. The fall mornings were cold; she was more of a heat girl. The warm weather made her feel comfortable. She didn't like the cold. She locked her car and walked into the apartment. She heard Alex in her room getting ready for the day. She didn't know if Brenda was up or not, so she wanted to keep quiet as she put her keys down on the table next to the door. She looked through the mail and she saw nothing really of importance to her. It was mainly bills and pamphlets. Being this close to multiple colleges caused a lot of junk mail to come to their house. Environmental pamphlets, political pamphlets, drug legalization pamphlets; Anne just found them annoying. The only thing of interest was a package for Alex.

She opened the internet bill and then the utility bill. She was fortunate in her situation. Her dad had bought the apartment as an investment. Anne didn't have to pay anything as long as she was responsible, Alex lucked out as the church paid for her bills, and Brenda was irresponsible in some ways, but she always paid her share of the food and bills. Anne grabbed the junk mail she collected and walked into the kitchen to throw it in the recycle bin. She was hungry so she went back to her usual quick meal, English Muffin with peanut butter and honey. Kale had introduced her to this quick breakfast, and she fell in love with it. She had it pretty much every morning with a cup of coffee and some sort of fruit. She sat down and started to read some of her notes for her class.

Alex came into the kitchen wearing her school uniform minus the blazer. Anne always found it amusing seeing her wear a Catholic school uniform with her long, black woven hair and dark make up.

"Morning," Alex said, grabbing an Apollo drink out of the refrigerator.

Anne replied back with a pleasant, "Good morning, how was your night?"

"Weird," Alex said. "I ran into a creature I hadn't seen since high school."

Anne's heart stopped, she immediately thought of Roger and that night where he had almost killed Kale and probably herself as well. If it wasn't for Alex and Komptin, Anne and Kale would not be here today.

Alex recognized the fear in Anne's eyes. "Relax," she said. "It wasn't Roger—not even an infiltrator." Alex grabbed a bowl and some kiddie sugary cereal. "It was that weird, misty thing that hung around Vandor."

Anne just watched Alex eat her cereal as she read the back of the cereal box. "You don't seem too worried about it."

"I've learned not to worry about such things, otherwise I drive myself insane," she said.

Anne could see that. A person must live their life, otherwise focusing on the bad will just drive a person over the edge. "You have always had a strong viewpoint on life. By the way, there's a package by the door. I saw it when I came home from Kale's dorm room."

"Oh, goody. I ordered these new sets of vacuuming seal bags. It's going to save a ton of room.

Anne just smiled at her.

"How's Kale?" Alex continued to read the back of the cereal box.

"He's fine," Anne answered. "I still think he is trying too hard and he wants to go back to where he was in high school. I can see sometimes his back and knees hurt him more than he tries to let on." Anne just shook her head.

Alex bit into her cereal, "Do you think I should tell him?" She continued to look at the back of the box.

"Tell who what?" Brenda asked, coming into the kitchen wearing skimpy pajama bottoms and a tank top.

"Telling Mole, I broke his sunglasses," Alex quickly covered herself. She was finishing up her cereal. She looked at her watch. "I need to get going." She put her bowl into the dishwasher and grabbed a piece of cooked steak from the fridge. Alex could see Brenda was looking at her. "It's for Komptin."

Anne heard Alex call for Komptin and the two of them left for school. Brenda grabbed the cereal still left on the table. "You know, I just don't know how like that girl can eat like she does and maintain being so skinny," Brenda commented. She put the cereal away and took an apple and yogurt and sat down across from Anne.

"Some people just have that ability," Anne said. She turned the page on her notes. Her phone chimed letting her know a message came in from Kale. She opened it to a picture of him in the shower covering his "Little Mole," as he liked to call it, with a bar of soap. Anne could feel her face turn red.

"What?" Brenda asked.

"Just a message from Kale," Anne said quickly, closing the picture.

"You know, Anne, he is, like, a real keeper. You better keep a tight rein on that one," she said, dipping her apple in her yogurt.

"We've been together since high school," Anne pointed out.

"Exactly my point," Brenda said. "You don't think being around those other girls over there got him tempted in straying?"

"Nope," Anne said in confidence as she turned the page of her notes.

"Like, don't ya think all men are the same?" Brenda asked her as she took a spoonful of yogurt. "I'm just saying none of them can be trusted."

Anne took her comments with a grain of salt. Brenda had a habit of picking the typical jock cliché. Those guys would hook up with her because she was an attractive girl, but really naïve. Anne believed the guys would get tired of her and then leave or cheat. At times, Anne really felt sorry for her.

"I need to get going to class," Anne said. "Have a good day."

***

Alex put the service dog harness on Komptin. She knew he hated it. It was necessary for him to wear it. The church pushed it through that he was her service dog. Alex never knew the justification they used, but she just told people she was severely anxious from an attack she had been in. It wasn't a total lie; she had been attacked numerous times. People normally didn't push because she had the scars to prove it. She clipped the leash on him. "Sorry," she scratched his ears.

They walked into the school building where she ran into one of the priests. "Alexandria."

"Father," Alex replied. Alex was not really in mood for a confrontation. Father Carl was not a fan of Alex. She never understood why. Alex maintained a "B" average, she was never late for any of her classes, and she was, for the most part, being good.

Father Carl just looked at Komptin. Alex could tell he was refraining from voicing his personal feeling about the dog being in the school. "I'm keeping tabs on you."

Alex was shocked, "Me? What did I do?"

"I don't know…yet. But I would like to talk to you after your first class," Father Carl told her.

Alex gave him a sarcastic smile back, "Can't wait."

"And watch that attitude young lady," he told her. "It's not the type of behavior we are known for or will accept if you ever want to graduate from this well-known prestigious school."

The first thing Alex thought of was, "I wonder if I'm on sacred ground?" She felt a small tingle in her arm as she could generate Lite. "Good to know," she said out loud.

"Excuse me?" Father Carl turned around.

"I said it was good to know that you think I have an attitude problem," she said to him. "Nice to know where I stand."

"We'll talk about this in my office after your first class," he said walking away, inspecting the hallway for cleanliness.

Alex looked up at the ceiling, "Just one time?" She lifted her finger in the air and lit it up. She playfully looked around for a sign of permission. "Didn't think so."

***

Sanah prayed in the corner of his little apartment. As he finished his prayers, he noticed that he could feel himself getting a bit hungry. He completed his prayer and rolled up his prayer rug to carefully put it away. This cherished rug had been given to him by his father when Sanah got married. He closed the door to the closet and had a sudden urge for some fried chicken. He never had it before coming to America, but he fell in love with the herbs and spices they used. He would order a bucket at least once a month. He placed the prayer rug in his room on the chair. He walked into the living room where he turned on the TV to watch an American Football team play, or as they called it, Soccer. He watched it and was amazed how bad the team actually was. His son could have beaten any of these "elite" American players.

He looked out the window where he saw how he missed the warm desert mornings. The morning sun caused the light to show neon pink in the sky. Here in America, the days just went from light to dark. Sanah walked into the bathroom to get ready to take a shower before he headed out. After he took his shirt off, he just sat and stared at each of his markings. Each scar on his body brought back flashes of the battles he had endured. Most of them were from infiltrators' claws digging into his body, the bad ones were from demons. It seemed each scar was a reminder of the life he had chosen. He closed his eyes and prayed.

He walked over to the table where he started to write a letter earlier in the day to his wife and son who were left in the warmth of the desert to continue his mission in America.

My dear,
Almost three months have
passed since I left the Holy Land
to fight on the new front. Each
passing day I think of your smile
and Assan's laugh, it helps me

*make it through the day. I know
a letter in this day and age
seems to be as ancient as the
war itself, but it adds a sense of
closeness to you. The time and
emotion I can put onto paper I
feel will be better transferred
onto you; it will show my love
for you and our son. I hope to
be home soon, I'm getting tired,
but I know what I do, I do it for
you and our child. My love will
be with you always.*

Sanah

Sanah found an envelope hidden behind some papers in the cabinet. He made a mental reminder to himself that he really should clean out his boxes and get things organized. He found a working pen and addressed the envelope, sealing it with a kiss. He put the letter in the inside pocket of his coat as he buttoned it up to protect himself from the cold. He wanted to make sure the letter got to its destination and the neighborhood he lived in caused him not to trust the inhabitants with such a sentimental item. Sanah tightened his coat as he got ready to head to the other side of town to mail his letter. He walked by a man giving a girl some white substance in a baggie. Sanah was hoping it was sugar for some baking she was doing but unfortunately, he knew what it was. He continued to walk as three other girls approached Sanah, asking if he was lonely. He kindly rejected them, hoping he didn't disrespect or offend them. A group of young males were playing loud music. They were cursing every other word near a stairwell. This was what the world was coming to.

He stopped at the bus stop waiting for it to arrive. He patiently looked down the street hoping to catch a glimpse of it. He really didn't want to stay there long. He could feel the air around him start to tense as people tried to stay their distance but not to make it look like they were. It was probably out of guilt knowing they shouldn't have such a prejudice against him for being Middle Eastern. He shrugged it off as he reminded himself he was chosen to help these people by fighting forces that they are completely ignorant of. He envied that.

Sanah managed to find an empty spot next to a young, pregnant woman. He smiled at her as he sat down next to her. She smelled of smoke and stale beer. He quietly prayed for the wellbeing of the child, knowing that the child was in for a rough life. He reached into another pocket and pulled out a book. He started to read a fantasy novel about dragons and wizards battling evil; something he could relate to. He double checked his letter to his wife and child before indulging in the pleasure of escaping to fantasy.

***

Alex waited outside Father Carl's office with Komptin on her side. The secretary just sat at her computer, continuing to type. The sounds of the keyboard were the only noise that was emanating within the office. Alex didn't even know why she was in here. She thought for sure that the church had cleared everything with school regarding Komptin. She started to pet her dog as she saw the secretary occasionally looking up at her.

She was in mid-to-late forties and from what Alex could tell she, too, was not a fan of Alex. Alex just mentally rolled her eyes as she went to her phone to text Anne that she was in Father Carl's office; for what, she did not know. Anne just replied with a sad face emoji with a "good luck" following. Komptin lifted his head up and looked to the door, giving Alex a warning that Father Carl was about to enter the lobby area. She started to grab her things as she got up to go into his office.

He opened the door, "You can leave them there, Ms. Johnson," he pointed to the chairs.

Alex took a quick second to regain herself as she put them down. She started to walk towards the office with Komptin following her.

"The dog doesn't need to come in either," Father Carl said.

Alex could feel her face start to turn red. She knew Father Carl was studying her to see what she was going to do next. The two seemed to stare at each other for what seemed to be an eternity. She decided not to say anything but just motioned to Komptin to sit by the door to wait for her. He laid down next to the door with his head up and ears perked. Alex could tell he knew that she was uneasy, and he didn't like it.

"Are we good with that?" she asked Father Carl. She honestly wasn't trying to start anything with him, but it naturally came out.

"You can leave that attitude out here as well. Now, come inside, young lady," he turned and sat behind his massive desk.

Alex sat down on the chair, getting ready for whatever was about to come.

"I didn't say you could sit," Father Carl told her, still standing at his desk.

Alex stood up and faced him. He looked at her and sat down. He grabbed his notebook and started to review some notes he had. She continued to stand looking at him, trying to see what he was looking at.

"Who is Father Tom Altomer?"

"He is the Administrative Priest that I report to," Alex said. "Why?"

"I will ask the questions," Father Carl informed her of the rules.

Alex started to look around the office. She couldn't believe she was in this office being treated as a delinquent of some sort. She noticed an old painting on an easel next to his library hutch. It was a young girl with a lighted sword fending off dark shadows. Behind her was a gated town with a man and his dog at the gates. She had to do a double take as the man in the picture had a resemblance of Osiah with Komptin. She tried thinking how she could get a picture on her phone of the painting.

Father Carl caught her staring at it. "The painting was found in an old church in a small town in England. The angel is protecting that peasant by the gates. The art department is going to clean it before being sent to the church that is sponsoring you."

Alex prevented a smile as she knew she was going to see that painting again. "Maybe the peasant is training her," she suggested. Memories of her former mentor raced through her mind when he was teaching her to survive this war.

Father Carl just shook his head out of disbelief. "You really have no sense of discipline in you, do you? You have no idea what true sacrifice is; to truly put yourself out there for something bigger than yourself," he scolded her. He just continued to stare at a folder with Alex's name on it.

"You mean like fighting a war and watching your family come close to death or failing to save the ones from the hand of pure evil itself? While continuing to fight an endless battle with no appreciation from those who don't even know it's happening...yep, no idea," Alex said to him as she continued to stare at the painting. Next to the painting was a hutch with pictures of a young Father Carl in uniform in a desert location.

Father Carl spoke, "Ever know anyone that served the Armed Forces?"

"No, not exactly," Alex informed him.

"I was in the Marines for 12 years, Chaplain Corp. I've seen a lot of people lose and gain their faith during war. God tests us, makes sure we maintain the course."

Alex snickered, "Really, that's what you think? He tests us?"

Father Carl lost his composure, "I spent my entire adult life serving Him and mankind. Who the blazes do you think you are?"

Alex was taken aback, "Father, I really don't know what you are talking about?"

26

"I see you don't have your dog with you," he pointed out.

"You told me not bring him in here," Alex said, raising her voice a little, pointing to the door.

"You tone down your voice when you are speaking to the Head Priest of this School!" he firmly raised his voice over hers. "Now sit down," he sternly commanded.

Alex sat down. She just wanted to Lite Beam Father Carl through the drywall.

"There's something I don't trust about you. St. Thomas Aquinas, a very big and respectable cathedral, sponsored you to come to this school, free of tuition, pushed that dog paperwork through for PTSD...doesn't really seem like you need it."

"The PTSD comes and goes," Alex's lip tightened.

"I'm not done. Now I, personally, was requested by Cardinal Joseph via Father Altomer to monitor your classwork, attendance, and how did he put it, general well-being," Father Carl looked at his notes before slamming them on the desk.

Alex just raised her eyebrows and looked to the side, full well knowing that the church was keeping tabs on her but she couldn't really say anything. "Maybe it's because they are paying my tuition that they feel they should know how their investment is."

"Investment?" Father Carl was shocked. "You really think you are an asset to the church? Possibly what could you do for our church?"

Alex tightened her lip and decided it would be best to keep quiet.

"When you get home, you look in the mirror; this long, black, fake hair, dark makeup, and wearing collars, and tell me if you see a good Catholic."

"I'm not Catholic," Alex pointed out.

Father Carl was on the verge of saying something he was going to regret. He took a moment to regain his self-control. "Ms. Johnson, I don't like the fact that you are taking a school slot that you didn't deserve; I've seen your high school transcripts. I don't like the fact that you have that dog in my school, I don't like the fact that you have some sort of special pull with a powerful church; and frankly I don't like your attitude."

"Is there anything you do like about me?" Alex asked him. She waited for an answer, but he didn't give her one. "Shocker."

"To put it bluntly, I don't think you belong here. Frankly speaking, I'm just waiting for you to screw up. Which I don't think it would be long," he told her. "Prove me wrong."

"You are a priest, right? I just want to make sure here," Alex said getting up. "I thought you people were supposed to give people chances." She looked at him right in the eye. "Are we done? Because I'd like to grab something to eat before I have to go to work tonight. You know, doing nothing to help the church."

"You're dismissed," Father Carl told her, going back to sit down behind.

Alex shook her head and left the office, shutting the door behind her. "Jackass," she said. She looked over at the secretary who was shaking her head with disgust at Alex. "Oh, bite me," she told the secretary. She gathered her things and walked out the door. She whistled for Komptin as he got up and followed her out of the building.

***

Alex and Komptin decided to walk through the park after class. It was a nice, brisk day and Alex wanted to enjoy the breeze and calm herself down. She strolled down the walking path where people were out with their tables trying to sell their agenda or even some merchandise. She stopped at a table which was selling leather products. She found a small, studded bracelet that was soft on the inside and pretty tough on the outside. It was a bit expensive, but she didn't mind paying for it. She was pretty sure the church would frown on her using the money they paid her to purchase such an item, but she didn't care. She was feeling a bit rebellious right now. It was against school policy to have that on in uniform so she made sure to show it off for everyone to see.

"Thank you," she said to the vendor. She turned around and was approached by a guy who definitely had his fair share of earthly herbs. "Excuse me," she said to him.

"Hey man, you wanna support our cause to legalize the greatest gift ever," he handed her a pamphlet. "The government just keeps illegal because they make money from the anti-pot programs." He raised his hands in the air. "Power the Pot."

Alex just shook her head as she took the pamphlet just to get him to shut up. She walked two steps until she was hit with another guy talking about how helping to rid the world of fossil fuels would save the planet for future generations. Alex was now getting annoyed; she grabbed the pamphlet and started to walk off. She then got hit with another person talking about how the wealthy one percent was keeping the ninety-nine percent suppressed while they got richer. Alex snatched the pamphlet and bumped shoulders with the guy, "Excuse me." She quickly got away. She looked down at Komptin, "I thought you were supposed to protect me." She then ran into another girl who approached Alex. She handed her a pamphlet with an upside down 4 on it. The initials F.O.R were on the cover. She seized the pamphlet and placed it with the others. "Ugh!" She grudged.

She finally got away from the crowd. She noticed a group of people leaving a table under a tree. She motioned Komptin to go seize it. Komptin ran to the table and jumped on it. He barked as he playfully guarded the table before Alex could join him at the table.

"Hey, get that dog off the table," a park attendant yelled.

Alex rolled her eyes. "Come on, boy," she said. "I don't need to have another authority figure mad at me for no reason." Komptin jumped down and found a place to lie down in the sun. Alex sat down at the table and pulled out an energy drink and a candy bar. She opened up her schoolbooks and read into her assignment.

Alex's nerves went up when Komptin raised his head and flashed his eyes. She looked around to her left, the right, behind her, and then out from the crowd she saw a beautiful, blonde woman approach her with two identical girls. It was Celestial with Ariel and Devine. They approached the table and Alex did a slow nod with her head.

"Hello, my child," Celestial said to her as she approached the table.

"Hello," Alex said, putting down her pen and standing up. "Ariel, Devine."

The two of them responded to her by a nod.

"It is nice to see you," Alex said. "It has been a while."

"It has, really has," she said. Komptin came up to Celestial. She knelt down to pet him. She generated something for him to eat from her hand. "Nice to see you both as well." She looked up at Alex who was staring at the people.

"Are you doing all right, Alexandria?" Celestial asked her, giving her a loving smile.

"Just a bad day at school," Alex told her. "Pretty much got in trouble for being a Lite Sentry." Alex saw Celestial look at her with a bit of worry on her face. "Don't worry, I didn't use my powers or anything, just life being difficult. Speaking of which, it can't be good if you are here," Alex commented.

"Actually, maybe you two can explain why we are here," Celestial looked back at Ariel and Devine.

The two of them hung their heads in shame. Devine spoke, "I wanted a churro."

Ariel then commented, "And I wanted a caramel apple."

Alex grinned, "Nice, I would have gone with the deep-fried Oreo myself."

Ariel and Devine looked at each other and gave each other a "why not" notion.

"Look out!" a boy yelled out as he was running towards Celestial. Alex just saw a Frisbee coming at Celestial's head. Ariel quickly caught the disc as Devine grabbed the boy, lifting him off the ground. "Oh crap!" the boy screamed.

"Shall I dispose of him?" Devine asked her mistress.

"It will be quick and painless," Ariel commented.

"Wait! What?" the boy asked in terror.

"Put him down," Celestial calmly said. She motioned for the boy to come to her. Celestial handed over the Frisbee. She looked into his eyes. "Here you go," she said to him. He silently thanked her. "And Michael." He turned around. "Love is closer than you think."

He smiled as he ran to a girl who was asking for him to throw the Frisbee back to her.

Alex smiled. "That was sweet. He's kind of cute," she said as she watched him run off to join what Alex thought was the girl Celestial was giving him advice on.

Celestial sat down next to Alex and picked up the pamphlets. She grabbed the one with the upside-down 4 on it. She opened it up and it read in bold letters "Freedom Off Religion." Alex could feel herself a bit embarrassed from having it.

"I can explain that," she pointed to it.

"No need," Celestial eased her. "I know where your heart is."

"Why are you here?" Alex asked her.

She looked to the sky where Alex knew Osiah's star would be. "I just wanted to see how you were doing." Alex put her head on the caring angel's arm. Celestial leaned her head onto Alex's head. She felt her Lite Sentry sigh as she closed her eyes. Celestial petted Alex's hair trying to sooth her as Alex stared out at the people in the park.

Chapter 2

Mole got done with his classes for the day. His back was starting to throb so he decided to sit down on the park bench. He caught himself watching people around the promenade, admiring the different activities each of them was doing. He saw the girl from his dorm this morning across the way. She was talking to a group of her friends as she kept on sneaking a peek at him. The girl waved to him after she realized she was caught. He returned the smile and waved back politely. Dan joined him after getting done with his accounting class.

"What's going on, big guy?" Mole asked. "Scoot those big cheeks on over here."

Dan sat down next to his friend, "Man, who knew accounting would be this difficult? T-brackets, debit this, but over here the same number is a credit...ugh!" He slammed shut the book and went to his sandwich. "This, my friend, this is what it is all about."

"The sandwich?" Mole asked while studying it.

"You know it. With every bite a person gets all four food groups. Dairy, grains, meats, and veggies; what more could you ask?" He took a big bite of food.

Mole adjusted his body, trying to get comfortable.

"You okay, dude?" Dan asked with a mouth full of food.

"Just trying to get comfortable," he answered. Mole sat back, looking into his bag for a banana he had left over. He found it all black and squashed over his paper. "Well, damn it." He held up what was left of his snack. "Thank God all I have to do is reprint my paper."

"Who's that?" Dan asked.

"Who?" Mole asked in return. Dan pointed to the blonde girl who smiled at Mole in the hallway. "I don't know. She came out of some guy's room early this morning."

"Well, she has been looking over here quite a bit trying to get your attention," Dan said, waving at her. She politely waved back but Dan knew she was hoping Mole was the one waving.

Mole looked up at her and she smiled, waving again. Mole smiled and waved back again. He turned to Dan who raised his eyebrows at him. "Don't even suggest it," Mole told him.

Dan replied, "Somebody got it bad for the Molster." Dan was making kissy faces at Mole.

Mole pushed his face away. "Well, there's a sight I hope to never see again," Alex said coming up behind Dan and Mole. "Mole, does Anne know about you and Dan?"

"She likes to watch," Mole instantly returned.

"Hey Alex," Dan said. He offered her a sandwich.

"Actually, I'm a bit hungry," Alex said, taking half and taking a big bite of it. "What are you guys doing?"

"That girl over there has a crush on Mole," Dan said, wiping parts of his sandwich from his mouth.

Alex looked over at the girl who was staring at her. She must have thought Mole and Alex were dating because the girl gave her a look of disappointment. "Who is she?"

35

"No idea," Mole said, looking at his phone.

Alex peeked at Mole's phone. The background had a picture of him and Anne snuggled underneath a blanket. "That's a cute picture of you and Anne."

Mole just stopped what he was doing and looked at Alex. "Alex, there is no way I would cheat on Anne." He put his phone down. "I would have to be the stupidest person in the world." He stood up to put his backpack on. "Besides, the way you two have grown over the last three years, you would kill me if I did anything to screw it up." Alex noticed he was pretty stiff. "I need to get going."

"You guys want to go to Distance Saturday night?" Dan asked.

"Sounds like fun," Alex said. "Can you and Anne go out?"

"I'll ask her if she wants to go," Mole said, grabbing his keys. "I gotta get going. Talk to you later, sis." He gave her a quick hug and punched Dan in the arm. "See ya, lover."

"Later," Dan said, finishing up his sandwich, blowing him a playful kiss.

Alex watched Mole walk over to his scooter. She could tell he was hurting. Feelings of guilt always rushed to her when she saw the moments he was hurting, not being able to do what he loved to do. He put his helmet on and drove off.

Dan gathered his items up as well. "I need to get going as well." He put his jacket on. "I've got to get to work. See you at the bar on Saturday."

Alex nodded in agreement and waved good-bye. She just wanted to sit and people watch as Celestial and she did earlier. It was a lie; Alex just

36

wanted to stay and see who this girl was. To her surprise, the girl came up to her. "This will be interesting," Alex thought to herself.

"Excuse me," she said to Alex.

Alex just stared at her, "Yes."

"Who was that?"

"Dan," Alex said watching him take off in his truck.

"No, the other guy," she corrected her.

"Why?"

"Well, I don't think the two of you are dating," she said to Alex.

The girl was starting to get an attitude with Alex, "Why do you think that?"

"He did not kiss you good-bye. It was a quick hug like a sister would get," she pointed out. "So, you're not dating or the worst girlfriend in history. Plus, you're really not his type."

"Really," Alex said, tightening her lips. Alex could use a pre-warm up fight before going out on a hunt tonight. Komptin came to Alex's side and barked at her. She just looked at him. "No, I'm not his girlfriend."

The girl smiled, "Good."

Alex wanted to wipe that pretty little manipulative smile off her face, "His girlfriend for the past three years is my roommate. So, I wouldn't get your hopes up. Besides, I really don't think you're his type," Alex waved her off.

The girl smiled at Alex, "I'm everyone's type. It's getting dark out soon, so I'm pretty sure your type should be getting out of their coffin anytime now." She turned around towards her friends, "Witch."

"Excuse me," Alex said, getting up.

Komptin barked again at Alex. She stopped to turn to her dog. "I wasn't going to hurt her...too badly." Komptin squinted his eyes at her. "Party pooper."

***

Mole went back to the dorm room to change to go to the gym. He put on a pair of shorts and his shirt but he needed a jacket because it was getting cold out. He went through his closet and noticed his Ironman Finisher Jacket hiding in the closet. He pulled it out to look at it. He had just realized he hadn't worn it since the night he got jumped by Roger.

Flashes of that night leaped into his mind. He quickly shrugged them off. He walked over to the mirror and put the jacket on. It still fit, and surprisingly, it was just a little loose. He was checking himself out when he heard the key in the door. Mole quickly took the jacket off and shoved it underneath his desk before Kameron came in.

"Didn't think you were going to be here," Kameron said. He went into his closet and put his jacket away.

"Class ended early," Mole said.

Kameron nodded, "Those are the nice days." He grabbed his books. "Well, I need to get moving if I am to graduate this year."

"Have a good study group," Mole said to him.

Mole got to the gym. He went into the pool where the swim team was finishing up their practice. Mole watched the team dive into the water and do practice drills. He changed into his swim gear and jumped into the lane that was only four feet deep. He carefully walked down the ladder into the water. He could only manage to walk up and down the pool for about 30 minutes before he would start to hurt.

He completed his workout and walked over to his scooter. He caught himself staring at the cross-country team running along with their coach on a bike yelling at them. He jumped onto his scooter. He had to drive the scooter because it didn't require him to push down with his feet. He had tried driving a car but pushing down on the gas hurt his back too much. Doctor said it was from the reconstructive surgery on his knee. Some tendon was pulling on another that was hurting his back. He tried a normal motorcycle, but he was having the same issue switching gears. So, his only other choice was a scooter. He strapped the helmet on and took off towards the room.

***

Anne got home before Alex and Brenda. She decided to take advantage of this time alone and jump in the shower for a nice, long, hot one. She was in the shower thinking about what Brenda said to her that morning. Would it be the fact that they haven't really had a serious relationship with no one other than each other that causes Kale to stray?

Anne's thoughts entered her mind. She had never thought like that, never in the past three years. She quickly changed her thinking. She knew she was most happy when she woke up next to him.

She knew sometimes it hurt him, but when he put his massive arms around her, she never felt so safe.

She had never been able to depend on another person before, but Kale was something different. She finished washing her hair and body. She stepped out of the shower, drying herself off.

She wrapped the towel around her and opened the door to a big guy in front of her. Anne screamed as she kicked the guy in the crotch. He went down, in pain holding his groin. The guy slowly got up, grabbing the towel, almost yanking it off Anne. She screamed as loud as she could.

The front door blew open as Alex came in with her fists glowing. Alex saw the guy attacking Anne. She didn't hesitate; she grabbed the guy and picked him up, slamming him onto the floor. Komptin charged through the doorway in full gargoyle mode with eyes glowing. Alex was about to strike when she heard a noise come from Brenda's room.

"Komptin," Alex said. "Watch him." Komptin morphed down to his dog state. Alex peeked into Brenda's room where she saw her roommate getting dressed for a date wearing headphones. Alex quickly diminished her fists and motioned for Komptin to let go of the guy.

The guy regained his composure. "What the hell?"

Alex picked him up, "Yah, that's my bad," she said, wiping dirt off his shoulders. The guy just looked at her in shock that a little, petite thing such as Alex picked him up like a rag doll and then threw him to the ground. "Turbo Boxing," Alex said to him, acting like a boxer. She went to check on Anne. "You okay?"

40

"Yah, I'm fine; he just scared me," Anne told her. She peered over Alex's body over at the guy. "Sorry."

He just grunted out of annoyance, trying to regain his strength.

Brenda came out, "What happened?"

"Nothing," the guy said. He got up and grabbed her hand to head out the door where he bumped into Kale. "Dude, wear a helmet?"

Kale played with the door, "Everything okay?"

Alex tried to think of an excuse, "Everything is good."

Anne adjusted her towel, "I need a couple of minutes to get dressed."

"Take your time," Kale said heading over to the couch. "What are your plans tonight?" he asked Alex who was grabbing her last Apollo out of her bag.

"Just studying, maybe go for a walk," Alex said, thumbing through one of Brenda's gossip magazines. They were cheap and mindless; Alex secretly loved them. She put down her magazine, "You okay?"

Kale turned on the TV. "Yah, I'm good. I've got a lot on my mind with graduation coming up next year."

Alex picked up her magazine, "Liar."

***

Sanah walked into the Mosque. This was only one of two temples that he could find. He wasn't surprised at the fact that this town didn't have that many. He removed his shoes and knelt down to

41

pray. He needed to pray extra today; he was missing his family and he knew he had a rough road ahead.

The mosque was nice, but it was too Americanized. He felt it was modernized unlike the authentic Middle Eastern mosques back in the Holy Land. After he finished his prayers he walked out to the streets. The air was chillier than what he was used to. He buttoned up his coat to keep the warmth close to him for as long as he could. It seemed to him no matter what he did, he always had a consistent chill in his bones.

He sat down on the bench in the park. The fall colors were turning the trees yellow with a hint of red trying to peek through. Sanah had read about the color changes of the fall. He would have to admit, the pictures he saw were truly amazing.

He made it back to his apartment where a little girl was playing in the hallway. The two just stared at each other. She was small and seemed to be very poor. He smiled at her, she smiled back. He grabbed ten dollars out of this pocket. He didn't want to insult her parents, so he put the money on the ground. "I seem to have dropped this." He winked at her. "I don't have time to look for it. I guess whoever finds it can keep it."

The little girl's face lit up. She quickly grabbed the money like a coyote grabbing food from a pack. She went running to her mother, holding her prize. Sanah watched the two of them through the door smiling as they cherished his minor gesture of compassion. Sanah didn't want to stare too long but seeing that moment of happiness was a rush of good feelings. It forced him on remembering how much he missed holding hands with his son walking in the goat fields. How he missed home. It was getting dark, as the streetlights were the main source of illumination. The air temperature seemed to drop a couple of degrees. Sanah buckled up his coat and started to walk towards the abandoned industrial park. It was dark, it heightened his nerves, and it was a prime location for infiltrators to be resting.

The first building he went through was cleared. There were a couple of signs of remains of what appeared to a homeless person's clothes. There were no signs of blood, though. There were no signs of any struggle. If the person allowed himself to be infiltrated, he would have stayed in the clothes he was in. The clothes were in a pile as if he or she had taken them off and left in that spot. He walked out of the building and walked into the main warehouse of a factory that had been left to rot for quite some time.

He couldn't really see what the products were made of in here, but there were chunks of metal and plastic all over the place. He slowly entered the room. He knew at least one of the horrific beasts was in there. He lit his blue fists when the two sets of red eyes appeared. He quickly prayed his supportive chorus and attacked into the darkness.

**

Alex took a shower before she went on her hunt. She liked to feel refreshed before she went out to find some of Vandor's minions. She wondered why she hadn't seen or heard from him since high school. Not that she was complaining.

His very presence had made her want to vomit. She knew that someday she would have to face him, plus she wanted to pay him back for what he did to Osiah.

The thought of Osiah made her feel kind of lonely. She was in this alone, but she was grateful for Komptin. She sat down on the bed next to her dog and scratched his head. "Shall we go for a walk?" Komptin lifted his head, flashing his eyes at her. "That's my boy," she said, playfully roughing him up.

Alex tied her long, braided hair in a ponytail and put on a black coat that reached down to her knees. She double checked her makeup because "a person cannot go out hunting looking like trash," she amused herself. She grabbed the collar she liked to wear to hide the scar from her battle with Sara's dad. She rubbed her fingers along the scar before covering it up with her black, studded collar.

The two hunters headed out into the urban jungle. It had taken Alex some time to teach herself to hunt in the city. For starters, she couldn't let Komptin go ahead of her and she really couldn't use her powers freely in fear of people seeing. Poor Komptin had to stay in his dog form for the majority of the time unless she came across some infiltrators.

The Council was very adamant about keeping their secret safe. Her only liaison to the Council was in D.C. now. She only contacted him briefly and in code via email or text messaging. Father Tom Altomer; she had to give him reports on a daily basis. He monitored her spending, and she had no idea who he was. She had never met him, and his messages were far from welcoming. Sometimes, Alex thought the Catholic Council was ashamed of her. She wished Father Joe would have stayed in contact. He was so nice and patient. The last time she saw him was at Osiah's funeral.

It was a nice little service that included herself and Father Joe, Celestial with Ariel and Devine, and another mystic figure named Malkaroy whom Alex had never seen before, but he was generally sad to say good-bye to Alex's former mentor. The ceremony didn't last long at all, but she remembered everyone had a sip from Osiah's flask and Celestial poured a little into a baby tree they had planted in the forest in honor of Osiah. She recalled Ariel and Devine didn't say a word during that time. They were there supporting Celestial who was maintaining her emotional strength. Alex herself broke down crying. She remembered being consoled by Komptin and Celestial. She had never felt such warmth run through her body like that night. It was as if Celestial had pushed a sense of love and content into Alex. That was the last time Alex saw Father Joe.

Alex and Komptin decided to get a bird's eye view of the land. She didn't really like hunting from up above because she couldn't really get into the feel of it. Tonight, was a different story; she wanted to look over the city at night. She got to the roof of a random building. The city was truly peaceful from up above. A couple of pigeons were roosting on a nearby sign. Komptin jumped on the ledge so he could see the streets below.

He nudged Alex to come see what he found down below. Alex looked down to see Anne and

Mole walking out of the restaurant. Alex watched; Anne was holding onto Mole's arm, tightly placing her head into it. Mole stopped and stared into her eyes as he leaned for a kiss. Alex observed the two embrace each other. Mole must have said something funny because Anne was laughing, hitting him in the chest. Alex caught herself smiling at the two of them. She was truly envious of their relationship; it would seem as nothing would get between them. "Come on, you peeping Tom," Alex said to Komptin. "Let's not be creepers."

Alex came across a church along the walk. They were hosting an AA meeting in the basement which meant the building was open. She walked into the sanctuary where she sat down in the middle of the pew, looking up at the crucifix. She just stared at it.

"Excuse me," someone said behind her. "Can I help you?"

Alex turned around to see an older man holding a tray of cookies. "Oh, I'm sorry," Alex said. "Am I not supposed to be here?"

"Not really," the man said. He walked up to her. His bright gray hair was emphasized by his dark skin. "Are you here for the meeting?"

Alex shook her head. "No, I just didn't feel like being alone tonight."

"Is everything alright? Do you want to talk?" the man asked. He had gentleness in his eyes. He must have been the minister of the church.

Alex shook her head no. "I just like the feel of the sanctuary, makes me feel safe as if no harm can come of me."

The man smiled, "Are you having scary thoughts?"

Alex laughed, "No sir, I'm not suicidal. I just feel a little lonely."

The man felt a little embarrassed and handed Alex a cookie. "Well, you don't look like you are going to cause any damage. You can stay here until the end of the meeting, which will be about an hour and half."

"I won't be that long," Alex informed him. "I just needed a second."

He nodded in acknowledgment. "I will be downstairs if you need to talk."

"Thank you," Alex said.

The man left for the meeting. Alex sat there closing her eyes. She wasn't tired, she was just enjoying the peacefulness. The light from Komptin's eyes caught her attention. She turned around to see Celestial sitting behind her, with Ariel and Devine in front of the church praying.

"Are they all right?" Alex asked. Celestial was watching the two guardians.

"They are just thanking Him for all He has given them," she said. "We all must do that once in a while." Celestial thumbed through the Hymnal. "He sometimes likes to know we still care."

"Will I ever meet Him?" Alex turned to her, still sitting on the pew.

"My child, is there something on your mind?" Celestial asked, putting the Hymnal down.

"It's stupid," Alex informed her. "I feel dumb just thinking it."

Celestial put her hands on Alex's arm which was lying on the top of the pew. "Please, you might feel better if you say it out loud."

"Well, I've known a lot of guys," Alex informed her. "I mean a lot."

Celestial smirked, "I know you have."

Alex just realized that was almost the first time she had seen her laugh. "Do you?"

"Do not ask questions which you do not want the answer to," she playfully replied.

"Fair enough," Alex said to her. "Anyway, they had never lasted more than a couple of nights before I ended the relationship." Alex looked down on the floor, "Am I incapable of love as a Sentry? Is it something I will never know?"

Celestial gazed up, trying to formulate her words, "I promise you; you will find a love in your future that you will not see coming."

"You know, don't you," Alex said.

She didn't answer. All she did was stand up and motion for Ariel and Devine to join her. Alex got up when Celestial did. Celestial put her finger on Alex's chest where her heart was. "Strongest I have ever seen," she told Alex. Alex watched her leave and then caught herself feeling lonelier than she did when she entered the church. Celestial stopped in her tracks and paused before turning around. "You will not see it coming," she smiled and went out the door followed by Ariel and Devine who just nodded to Alex as they followed their mistress.

Alex looked down at Komptin who was sitting up next to her, "Damn it, why the hell are you "all powerful" beings so damn cryptic?"

Ariel and Devine popped their heads around the corner of the doorway, "Language," they both said.

***

Salamor floated along the sides of two infiltrators. He walked into the warehouse where he had felt the Lite Sentry's presence. He sniffed the air. "She was here," he said to the infiltrators. Salamor knew there had been a battle, but he did not see the remains of the Sentry, which meant she had won the fight. Salamor was shocked she managed to take on the infiltrators that were there. He knew there must have been at least four of them in the building alone. The two infiltrators that were at his side were scuffling near the corner of the wall. Salamor commanded them to move. The two of them scattered in fear as he approached a small pool of human blood. Salamor put his face close to the blood and sniffed it. "This is Lite Sentry blood." He told them. He put his finger in the blood and placed it in his mouth. "This is not her blood." He floated to the window and looked outside to the window where he saw a man extinguish his blue fists walking down the parking lot. "Sanah is here."

Chapter 3

Sanah walked through the park on his way home for morning prayers. The door creaked as he entered his apartment. He hated living here but it was close to where infiltrators liked to find their victims. He saw the little girl from yesterday playing again in the hallway with an old Barbie doll and a rundown box as a house. She had bags underneath her big brown eyes. Sanah had stopped off at a bakery prior to coming home. He placed a twenty-dollar bill in the bag with a couple of bagels. He slowly walked over to the girl and handed it over to her. He placed his hands gently on the child's head and smiled. She looked at him with tears of joy as she got up to show her mom who now stood in the doorway watching him. He smiled at the mom as she looked inside the bag. He just nodded and went back to his apartment.

He had to hurry and wash prior to prayer. He took off his jacket and shirt and looked at the wound where an infiltrator swiped at him. It got a good chunk out of him, but it was no worse than he had before. He quickly bandaged it up and went to pray. The sun rising from the window filled the room with a warm heat. He took a minute to enjoy the sun and thank Him for all He has done. He prayed for forgiveness of his sins and protection to his wife and child. That morning, he needed to spend a little more time in the sun for Morning Prayer.

***

Alex finished her shower and got into her comfortable, thick, white bathrobe. She walked into the kitchen and grabbed her sugary cereal. She sat at the kitchen table eating her breakfast while drinking her Apollo energy drink. It was pretty early, and Anne walked in her bathrobe as well. She seemed to have an extra spring in her step.

"Morning," Alex said, not missing a beat while reading the back of the box.

Anne got herself a cup of coffee, "Thanks for the coffee."

"I didn't make it," Alex said.

Brenda walked in the kitchen wearing her clothes from the night before.

Anne and Alex looked at each other and smiled. "Just getting in?" Alex asked.

"He's the one," Brenda said. "I know it." She giggled as she got a cup of coffee. "I would like to get ready for work but I'm so tired," She giggled again and left for her room.

Anne just shook her head. "That girl falls in love every other week."

Alex muttered underneath her breath, "At least she can."

"What was that, sweetie?" Anne asked her as she got yogurt.

Alex shrugged it off and continued to eat her cereal. "So not that I'm stalking you or anything, but I saw you and Mole come out of Antonio's last night."

Anne smiled as she looked through her phone at the news. "Where were you?"

"Rooftop overlooking the city," Alex said. "Purely coincidental."

"Sure," Anne teased. "Alex, can I tell you something?"

"Of course," Alex said. She put down the cereal box to give Anne her full attention. "What is it?"

Alex could see Anne was having trouble saying what she wanted to tell her. "You have to promise not to tell Kale."

"Not a word," Alex said.

"Promise me," Anne pleaded with her.

Alex lit her fingers in her neon blue mist and crossed her heart, "I promise."

"Alex, I love him. There's no doubt about it. I am truly, deeply, in love with him," Anne admitted. "He makes me laugh; he comforts me when I'm down. He values my opinion, he respects me, and when I'm not near him I think of him."

Alex just sat back in the chair. "Anne, it's almost been over three years since you've been together, you never said anything?"

"I wanted to make sure it wasn't just, you know, lust," Anne admitted. "But there is no doubt about it, I am in love with Kale Moler." Anne laughed at herself. "Who would have guessed? I couldn't stand him in high school up to that night at the lake, then it all changed."

"What happened that night that changed your mind?"

"He got rid of Roger and then gave me a sweatshirt because I was cold," Anne said. "That simple gesture made me look at him in a new light.

He got rid of him and then he just stayed with me and we just clicked."

"Has he said it to you?" Alex asked.

"You know Kale, he hides everything serious about himself with humor or keeps it bottled."

"I have known Mole for a long time; since grade school we've hung out together," Alex said. "Even when it was revealed we are brother and sister, we still had a close bond and I will say this: that bond between us is no comparison on how he feels about you."

All Anne could do was smile with her eyes starting to water.

"Why are you crying?" Alex asked.

"I'm just happy," Anne admitted, wiping away a tear.

"Oh my God," Alex got up from her chair and hugged Anne. The two were holding each other when Brenda walked in.

"Oh, you guys, I can't believe you are so happy for me you're, like, crying over it!" she said, hugging the two of them.

Alex rolled her eyes.

***

Mole finished up his walk in the lap pool. His physical therapist was watching him from the other end. Mole got out of the pool as the air was a bit nippy. He hugged himself as the therapist met him with a towel.

"How's it going?" he asked.

"I feel good, Randy," Mole told him.

"Any pain?"

"Nope," Mole answered him. "Do you think I could try running?"

Randy was battling the answer in his head, "Have you tried running?"

"Tempted, but not tried," Mole said. "Come on. I need to do more."

"I don't think it's a good idea," Randy said. "Let me go look at the latest x-ray and we should talk about this in my office after you get dressed."

"Ok," Mole said. He got into the locker room and finished his shower. He was putting his pants on and staring at the scar on his knees. The feeling came back to him of Roger swinging that baseball bat at his knee cap. That changed his life forever. The sharp sensation shooting up through his back telling him he would never race again. He put his leg down and jumped up to get his pants on. When he landed, he felt his right, lower back give out. He fell into the locker, as a sharp pain pulsated. He gripped the door of his locker, trying to pull himself up. He fought back from crying out loud as he lay down on the locker room bench.

He managed to pull himself into Randy's office door. He knocked and walked in and sat in the chair. "Come on, give me some good news."

Randy reviewed his chart and looked at Mole. "You okay? You look pale."

"Cold from getting out of the pool," Mole lied to him. "What do you think of me running again?"

"I don't think it would be wise. Your knees have some serious damage and your L5 is weak," Randy said. "You can try swimming."

Mole fought back from anger, "What if I try running no more than a mile?"

"Tell you what, you give me 100% in your water workouts and we will seriously look into running for you," Randy suggested.

"In other words, no on the running," Mole interpreted.

"It's just not a good idea," Randy told him.

"I understand," Mole said. He got up with a shot of pain coming to his back. He tried hiding it but he was pretty sure Randy caught it.

"Try to keep positive," Randy said. "I'm here if you need to talk."

Mole nodded as he left Randy's office. He got to his Scooter parked outside. He hated that Scooter; it represented everything he couldn't do. He couldn't take Anne anywhere, she had to drive everywhere, he couldn't ride his bicycle, he couldn't run, he couldn't be Mole. He put his helmet on and started up the bike.

***

Anne was getting ready to go out to Distance. It was a dance club where a lot of college kids hung out. The club was known for their theme nights. Once a month, they had either an 80s night, 70s, Techno, country, etc. Anne couldn't remember what tonight's theme was. She never dressed for the themes, she just loved looking at other people's costumes for the night.

Anne finished fluffing her hair as she put her flower in her hair. She opened the door to see Alex sitting on the couch, reading a gossip magazine. "Are you coming with us tonight?"

"I don't know," Alex said. "I was going to go for a hunt."

Anne peered to see if Brenda was home. Usually Alex said, "Walk" which was code for "hunt" in case anyone else was around.

"She isn't here, she went out with that guy you kneed in the nuts last week," Alex informed her. "You are really making a habit out of that."

"Twice, only twice," Anne said, putting up two fingers. "Why don't you come out with us?"

"Probably would be a good idea for me to get some relaxation," Alex said. "Komptin."

Komptin came out of the room and joined Alex on the couch. "We are taking the night off. I'm going to go out." Alex could see he wasn't too keen on the idea of leaving Alex's side, but he reluctantly agreed. "Sometimes I wonder who is in charge between the two of us." She kissed him on his head.

"Give me a couple of minutes to get dressed," Alex said. "How is Mole getting there?"

"Dan is bringing him," Anne said, sitting down next to Komptin on the couch. Komptin laid his head on Anne's lap. She really didn't mind because Komptin never shed a single piece of fur.

"Are you going to tell Mole how you feel?" Alex yelled from her room.

"Not tonight," Anne yelled back. "I really don't think a loud dance club is a place for that."

"I can see that. I would get pretty annoyed if somebody did that to me," Alex said. Alex put on her black skirt with black tights. She found a pink and white studded skull shirt Mole got her for her birthday, which actually reminded her. "Hey Anne, we should treat Mole out to a nice dinner for his 21st birthday."

"Not a bad idea," Anne said. "I was trying to think of something special to do since he can't drink."

"Where do you think we should take him?"

Anne came back with the perfect answer, "What about Zion's?"

Alex came out of the room after applying her dark makeup. "You know, that is a good idea."

"I'll make the reservations," Anne told her out of excitement.

***

Alex and Anne met up with Dan and Mole in the parking lot of Distance. Mole was looking around at the people dressed in neon colors with what looked like pipes and leather straps acting as hair. Some people also had gas masks on their face, wearing fluffy feet bottoms.

"What the hell is going on here?" Mole asked, looking around. "Hold me, Dan, I'm scared." He grabbed onto Dan, giving him a big hug.

"We're all scared, son," Dan answered back, looking around, returning the hug.

Alex's face lit up, "This looks like fun!"

Anne and Mole grabbed hands, "Just remember, this was all Dan's idea," Mole told the group.

"Oh, relax, you big baby," Anne told Kale. "Keep your mind open. Good things come to people who open their eyes," she smiled at Kale.

"Let's do this!" Dan said. "They still better be selling PBR here."

They got inside and the music was blaring. Every beat of the bass was causing their clothes to vibrate. The place was packed, and its people seemed to be having a very good time. Kale found a seat in the back corner while Alex, Anne, and Dan went to the bar.

Alex ordered, "Two Apollos, one club soda, a glass of wine, and," Alex looked over to Dan who just nodded, "and a PBR." The bartender looked at her and then got her the drinks.

Alex had her drinks and walked by the dance floor which was a sea of neon colors dancing all about. Alex was in the mood to dance. She placed her drinks with Mole and headed out to the dance floor.

She screamed as she entered the dance floor. She found her rhythm and was in pure bliss. There were two girls up on the rafters in neon pink. They were dancing very close to each other. The two of them had pink and white leather straps for a wig, wearing a pink tube top and hot pink tights with white skirts. The two commanded the attention they deserved.

Alex danced and danced. She felt a guy coming up behind her. She turned around to see a guy with dyed, neon red hair. He wore a red leather jacket with the sleeves cut off. His black leather pants moved in compliance with her hips. Alex wrapped her arm around his neck as the two danced to the music.

***

Mole watched Dan talking to what Mole could only guess was a girl. The three of them were definitely not in their element. Mole wanted a refill of his club soda but really didn't feel like getting up. He knew that if he got up it was going to hurt. He scooted over to the edge of the booth and forced himself up. He motioned to Dan who now was making out with the girl. Dan just gave him a thumbs up without even looking at him.

Mole managed to get to the bar and was feeling better as he walked up to it. Anne had to go to the bathroom, so he was there among the neon leather and gas masks all by himself. Two girls joined him in line at the bar. They were both wearing pink, looking over at Mole.

"Oooo, we got a curious one," one of the girls said.

The two girls had each other's arm, licking their lips over in Mole's direction. "He's kind of cute for a dude," the other girl said.

They seductively looked at Mole for the first time in quite a while and didn't know what to say. He just smiled and said, "Sorry, ladies, my heart belongs to another."

The two of them at the same time replied, "Oh bummer."

Anne joined Kale in line at the bar by holding his hand. She looked back at the girls in pink. "Hello."

"Oooo, she's cute," one of the girls said.

"They look good together," the other one said.

Anne genuinely smiled at them, "Thank you."

59

Alex came up to Anne and Kale with some guy. "Hey, do you guys want to get out of here?"

Mole looked up and down at the guy dressed like he was Michael Jackson reject, "Go where?"

"I'm hungry," Alex said. "Oh, this is Gastrix."

Mole did everything in his power not to laugh. He felt Anne's fingernail dig into his hand.

Anne stuck out her hand, "Hello, Gastrix. I'm Anne and this is my boyfriend, Kale."

"You mean like the green leafy garnish on my food plate," Gastrix said snickering.

Kale forced a smile as Anne's fingers dug deeper into his hand. "Yes," he looked over at Anne. "Shall we grab Dan?"

Anne looked around, "Where is he?"

Dan and the girl that he was kissing headed out the door. She had her hand down the back of his pants. "That is a brave woman," Kale pointed out.

The two girls in pink were whispering to each other as they licked each other's ears. They blew kisses at Mole and Anne. "Come again, we'll be here."

"Okay let's go," Alex said. Gastrix held her hand, guiding her through the crowd.

Anne and Kale started to walk out together when they were stopped by the two girls in pink. "Watch your friend," one of them said.

"He's not a nice man," the other finished.

"Thanks for the advice," Mole said, looking over at Gastrix with amazement that Alex ended up with him.

Anne handed them her drink voucher, "There are four drinks on here, please have it."

One of the girls grabbed it and sniffed it. "You're sweet."

***

Anne and Kale walked out of the dance club, watching Alex with Gastrix next to Anne's car. "What do you think?" Anne asked Kale.

"I think Alex will see him tonight and we will not hear from him again," Kale grabbed the keys to the car. "I guess I'm driving." He flipped the keys in the air.

Anne liked it when Kale forced himself to drive. She knew he couldn't drive long distances, but he could do it for short distances. After twenty minutes of straight driving, he started to get pain in his back. "Please tell me Dan is coming with us."

Mole got a text from Dan. He opened it to see a picture of Dan shirtless with a cyber girl topless and licking his ear. "I doubt it." He showed the message to Anne. "Gross, isn't it?" Anne playfully pushed Kale in the arm.

She laughed, "Good for Dan."

"I was talking about riding with 'Gastrix'," Kale air quoted.

"Best smiling faces, dear," Anne reminded him. The two of them walked up to Alex who was pinned up against the car, being kissed by 'Gastrix'. "Where do you guys want to eat?"

"I'd love to have a double cheeseburger from Ronnie's," Alex suggested.

"Oh no, you have to have this veggie burger from a non-franchise place I know," Gastrix said.

"They are still open." He opened the door to the backseat as he got in first. "Come on, Alex."

Alex laughed as she slid in next to him. Anne dug deeper into Kale's hand, "Ow," he said to her. "Is that for your benefit or mine?"

"Let's go get this over with," Anne said.

***

"Dearest Love,

This mission is getting more difficult. I keep on coming across this little girl and her mother. I give them what money and food I can to help them. The little girl's eyes are nothing but pure innocence. It reminds me so much of Asaan's big, wide, brown eyes. My hunts are getting more productive but there is a cold evil in the air. It scares me, it scares me to think about failure. I'm getting tired, honey. The only thing I know is my love for you and Asaan is strong.

Sanah came out of the post office after dropping off the letter to his home. He started to make it a point to bring some food and money to the little girl from his apartment building. He found the little girl's smile a nice little motivator to keep him going in his long fight.

62

He found the little girl in the hallway again playing with her doll. He walked ever so quietly and handed her a bag of fruit and a 50-dollar bill. He didn't say a word to her. He never did. He just smiled and left, knowing what little he did was making a difference in their world and that is what kept him going.

Chapter 4

The pain from his back woke Mole up from what little sleep he was getting. He tried to lie still so Anne could get some sleep so he really couldn't get comfortable. He carefully rolled out of bed, being careful not to wake her up. He grabbed his phone and headed out to the living room. He stopped off at the bathroom to grab some pain medication. He opened the bottle and thought he had more than what was there. Mole tried to recall how many times he popped the pills. A panic came over him because he was afraid he was falling back into addiction. He quickly shut the bottle and put them back into the cabinet. He just figured he would take some Ibuprofen to help ease the pain. He knew he wouldn't be addicted to that.

He finished in the bathroom and walked out to the living room. He looked over the couch to see Komptin laying down pretty much covering the whole thing. "What are you doing out here, boy?" Mole laughed because it actually looked as if Komptin was annoyed as he looked to the bedroom where Alex and 'Gastrix' went into bed. "Scoot over," he said to the massive dog. He sat down and Komptin placed his head on Mole's lap. Mole slowly scratched the dog's ears. "Looks like we are both in for a long day, huh?" Mole laid his head back on the couch as he heard the door open. Normally, he thought it would be Alex getting in from her walk, but Komptin was still on the couch. He watched the door open as Brenda came stumbling in, clearly intoxicated. It looked like she had been crying. "Are you okay?" Mole asked.

"That guy you met yesterday dumped me," she broke down. "It's like, I don't get why people do that."

Mole knew this was a mistake, but his conscience wouldn't allow him not to do it, "What happened?" He cringed inside his body.

Brenda jumped at the opportunity and sat down. She started crying, "He told me that he needed somebody on the same intellectual level for him to reflect with," she sobbed. "I don't even know what he meant by that!" She continued to cry.

Mole wanted to get out of the situation, but he couldn't find a way. Luckily, Anne came out. She came up behind Kale and gave him a hug with a kiss on the cheek. "Everything all right?"

He whispered to her, "Brenda's man friend broke up with her."

Anne patted Kale on the shoulder, telling him she was going to take care of it. Anne asked Brenda if she wanted to talk about it.

"Yes," Brenda sobbed.

"How about I cook you breakfast?" Mole offered. "How about an egg-white omelet with green peppers and onions."

"Are you going to want to kiss me after that?" Anne teased.

"Nothing can ever prevent that," Kale said, kissing her.

***

Anne and Kale had finished eating breakfast when Alex walked into the kitchen. Anne noticed how Alex had a strange smile on her face. A look Anne had seen before, usually after a night with a guy. If Alex stuck with tradition, this guy would be gone by lunch.

"Morning," Kale said, finishing up his orange juice. "You look, I guess, happy."

Alex blushed, "It was a good night."

Mole put up his hands, "Don't want to hear about it. Sorry, I didn't know you were up otherwise I would have made you some eggs."

"No big," Alex went into the cupboard to grab some of her sugar cereal. She poured her cereal and sat down. "I think I found a good guy."

Mole spit out his orange juice and Anne immediately kicked him underneath the table. "Sorry, went down the wrong pipe."

Anne handed him a napkin, "Why do you say that, sweetie?"

"He's just a good guy. We have a lot in common. Music, style, both night owls, and he shows me stuff I've never done. You know we just connect," Alex admitted.

"You've known him just for," Anne looked at her watch. "Under 12 hours."

"I just know," Alex said.

"I can understand that philosophy," Anne said, looking at Kale who was trying to ignore the conversation by reading his phone. "But are you sure it's not something else?"

The door opened to Gastrix coming into the kitchen. He opened the fridge acting like he'd been living there for years. Anne watched him as he

66

scouted the fridge. He turned to see what Alex was eating. "You really shouldn't be eating that."

"I know it's not good for me, but it tastes so good," Alex said, biting into the cereal.

"You're going to get fat," Gastrix abruptly told her.

Anne raised her eyebrows as Kale was obviously biting his tongue. Anne decided to speak before Kale said something that was going to start a whole bowl of drama, "So, where do you work?"

"I'm currently mixing music, selling it online," he informed him.

Kale couldn't help himself now, "Are you making a pretty good living off of it?"

"Man, I don't do it for the money. My music is to spread the message," Gastrix informed him.

"And what message is that?" Kale asked, putting down his phone, giving his full attention to him now.

"The message of how installations around the world are suppressing the rights of individuals and forcing them to believe in their ridiculous ideals," he preached.

"Well, how do you pay for food and a place to live?" Kale asked.

Anne placed her hand on Kale's leg and dug her fingernails in. Kale's phone vibrated. He picked it up and read it. Anne watched him laugh. "What's going on?"

"Dan sent me a picture of him and that girl he picked up last night," Mole showed Anne the picture of Dan giving thumbs up with a girl laying on his chest, out cold.

"Well, I guess I should get into the shower before Brenda uses all the hot water," Kale said, getting up. "Gastrix," Mole formulated his words, "It's been enlightening."

Alex spoke up, "Unless you want to do something tonight?"

"Like what?" Gastrix asked.

"How about we go to a movie and ice cream afterwards?"

"Sounds like a teen date, plus that's a lot of junk food that you don't need," Gastrix said. "Let's go see this dance club that I know of."

"Okay," Alex enthusiastically told him.

Kale thought for sure she was over emphasizing her excitement as if trying to convince herself it was something she wanted to do.

"It's Sunday," Kale reminded him. "Really, on a Sunday?"

"I don't know days, man," Gastrix told Kale.

Kale just shook his head and got up from the table.

***

Sanah finished his afternoon prayers and tended to his wound. It was healing nicely but he knew this was going to be another scar to add to his collection of historic battles. He slowly removed the bandage. There was still a little blood oozing from the open areas, so he had to replace the bandage with a fresh one.

He turned on the television to watch American style football. He never understood the draw to it. Sure, it was brutal, but for what he could tell they hardly ever used their feet in the game. There seemed to be no finesse to the sport, just a bunch of barbarians trying to overpower each other.

Sanah shut the television off and stared out the window. The nights were coming sooner than the day prior. This meant his hunts were to be longer. He sure missed the relaxation of sleep. He forgot what it was like to dream. He couldn't even remember what his last dream was before he accepted the Lite Sentry mission. He stared as he watched the sun set over the city. He pulled out the chair to the kitchen table to finish up his letter to his wife.

> *The nights are getting longer and longer. I'm running into more infiltrators than expected. I have heard that the Lite Sentry in South America has been hunting more in deep jungles versus within the town. I wonder why they are so interested in this American city. It's dark here, really dark. On top of it, the cold is coming to my bones. I wish I could feel the warmth of you and Asaan overlooking the fields. Soon, soon I will be with you.*
> *Love Always,*
> *Sanah*

He put on his coat to head out the door with a bag in his hand. Sanah got to their door and he softly knocked on the door and the little girl opened it. To her surprise, in the bag was a thick sleeping bag, multiple cans of soup, and a stuffed toy lion. Again, no words were exchanged; just the appreciation in the girl's eyes communicated all that needed to be said.

***

Alex was in her room watching Gastrix sleep next to her. She didn't know how she could keep her secret of not being able to sleep which would in turn lead to her admitting to being a Sentry. Maybe she should tell him? After all, Alex knew he was the one. "This was the one Celestial must have been talking about." She laid in bed with him for a couple of hours, being careful not to disturb him. She was able to get out of bed without disturbing him and was looking at what to wear for her hunt tonight. She was hoping not to run into any infiltrators because she knew Gastrix wanted to go to that club.

She quietly picked out her clothes and headed into the bathroom to change. She came out of the bathroom to Gastrix tossing and turning. "Where are you going?" he moaned. Alex could tell he was irritated but that was probably because she was not next to him. She thought she was lucky to have a man who wanted her so much.

"I'm going to take Komptin for a walk," she said, coming up to the edge of bed and looking at him. "I will meet you at the club."

"How am I supposed to get there if you're not here," he asked, burying his head into the pillow.

"I'll leave you some money for a cab on my dresser," Alex told him. She dug into her wallet and laid some money down for the cab. She kissed him on the forehead. Alex slowly closed the door to Komptin sitting down, looking at her outside her door. "You ready?" He was moving slower than usual to the outside door. "What's wrong, boy?" He looked up at her with his big brown eyes. "I know what will make you feel better. Let's go see what kind of trouble we can get into." Komptin started wagging his tail out of excitement. "The faster we find them, the sooner I can make it to the club." Alex walked out the door with Komptin's excitement diminishing.

***

It was approaching ten at night when Sanah came across signs of a couple of infiltrators. There was no doubt about it, they were out and looking for a kill tonight. Sanah could always tell by the feeling of the air. There was no point to the infiltrators if they didn't inhabit a person, so they just killed. They were absolutely horrible creatures. A product of pure evil. He picked up the trail leading towards a group of abandoned buildings. Sanah couldn't help but find himself relieved the trail was heading away from the little girl and her mother at his apartment. The sense was getting stronger as he continued to follow the trail.

The path the infiltrators took was leading into a high crime area where drugs, prostitution, and homelessness were abundant. Infiltrators liked the homeless for a quick kill because they were forgotten. A missing homeless person was not a big concern to the local authorities. "The sin of man causes so much heartache," he thought to himself. That is why he fought, to make it better. He found that the trail was leading into another warehouse. Sanah entered the area but there was something different in the air. The energy in the building was different. He did not like the sense of this hunt. There was something amiss. He did not like where this was going. Something was about to change.

***

Alex and Komptin were enjoying their walk when Alex picked up the sense of an infiltrator. She looked down to Komptin and he verified the scent. Alex almost felt a sense of disappointment when she picked up the trail. She knew she was going to be late for her date with Gastrix. Komptin started on the trail and it led through the park. Alex could feel that the infiltrator hadn't found a willing body to inhabit, which meant they were out for the kill.

Alex always wondered what would be worse, being killed by an infiltrator or being possessed by one. She knew the only way to rid a person who was possessed by an infiltrator was to kill both of them together. She only ran into two people who accepted the infiltrator, Roger and Sara's dad, Jim. Roger was still out there, but Jim was eliminated the night Sara died. Alex got the scar on her neck as a constant reminder of it. The only comfort Alex had about that night was Sara was no longer in pain, she was at peace. Alex missed her friend.

They left the park and ended up in the poor side of town. A strange man approached Alex. "Hey, you looking to party?"

Alex replied, "No, thank you." She continued to walk until the stranger grabbed her arms and twisted her around. "Hey!"

"You are pretty daring walking through here at night, let me take care of you," the man said, pulling her closer to him. Komptin turned around, flashing his eyes and morphing into his gargoyle state, growling before letting loose a massive deep bark that echoed through the air. The man let go of Alex, slowly backing away. Komptin lunged after him until Alex grabbed him around his neck. The man turned to run but ran into a lamp pole, knocking himself out.

"What has gotten into you?!" Alex said, trying to calm Komptin down. Komptin morphed back into his dog form, giving the man a dangerous stare. Alex crouched down to check on the man. She turned around to scold Komptin, "You are damn lucky he's alive." Alex made sure no one else was around. "And that no one saw us. Come on." She angrily walked off before stopping and kneeling down to Komptin who was lagging behind. "I'm sorry, boy. He couldn't have hurt me and you're lucky he was high as a kite because if he identified you, we'd both be in a situation the Council would not be fond of..." She let go of him. "I just don't want to lose you." She motioned for him to follow as she continued on her hunt. "Come on."

Alex looked at her watch. She knew she had an hour before she had to be at the dance club. She would never abandon her hunt when she was on the trail, but she also knew Gastrix was going to be upset if she stood him up. The consequences if she left her hunt would be the death of an innocent soul. "It looks like it leads into that warehouse." She continued down the path to the entry door. "Sweep the perimeter, I'll go in for look-see." Komptin flashed and morphed into his gargoyle body. He took off as Alex wished. She looked at her watch again. "Man, I'm going to be really late." She entered the dark entryway to the warehouse. She got a vibration on her phone with a message from Gastrix saying he was at the club and he wanted her there. She turned her phone to silent to ensure the infiltrators knew she was present. There was something else in the air. Something out of the ordinary.

***

Sanah was on the top floor of the warehouse. He knew the infiltrators were somewhere in this massive room. He didn't know how many were in the room, he just knew they were in here. Normally, he would light his fists and attack, but there was something he never felt before in the air. He couldn't place it. He slowly walked into the room. It was dark, and he made himself available for an ambush, so he drew out whatever was near. Sanah took a couple of steps when he saw five sets of red eyes appear out of the darkness. He stood still in the room staring down at the fight he was about to endure. It wasn't the most he'd ever fought at once, but a little bit more than usual.

***

Alex ran up the stairs to the top floor. She knew that Komptin would be finishing his perimeter search and would be covering the bottom floor, working his way up. The two of them would meet in the middle. Alex got to the top of the stairs where she sensed the infiltrators nearby. She also knew Salamor was close as well. She knew what his sense was. She didn't fear Salamor because he was more of a nuisance than anything. He could not be touched but in turn, he could not harm anyone corporeal. The only thing he could do was give negative suggestions to people who were willing to listen. Alex knew she was too headstrong for anyone to manipulate her. That sense she knew, the infiltrators she knew, but there was something different.

Alex continued to walk down the hall where she saw a service door open into the main room of the floor. She slowly crept up to the door where she peered around the corner. She couldn't believe what she saw. Multiple sets of eyes in the dark staring at a man standing in the middle of the floor. They must have brought him back here to tear him to shreds and feed on his fear.

She had never taken on this many infiltrators before by herself. She knew she had to protect the man. She only hoped Komptin would make it up to the floor in time to help. She said a quick prayer and lit her fists. She lunged into the dark room full mode, ready for battle.

Alex jumped in front of the man and pushed him out of the way, "Go on; get out of here!" she yelled at him.

***

Sanah could not believe what he was seeing. There was another Lite Sentry here. He had not gotten word that another one was activated. He knew of the one in South America but not in America. She was small, petite with pale skin and her braided, black hair was long. Sanah couldn't help but think on how that must get in the way. She commanded the room as she stood her ground. He thought she must have had multiple battles because she leaped into the heart of a five on one battle. Normally, Sanah would have identified himself right away, but his curiosity had gotten the best of him; he wanted to see what she could do.

***

Alex looked behind her again, "What in the hell are you waiting for?" The man just stood there. She figured he was stunned by the presence of such creatures. Alex didn't have time to run and protect this guy. She knew she wasn't going to last long without Komptin at her side. If she was going to fall tonight, then she was going to take some of these bastards with her. Hopefully he would get enough sense and start to run.

They charged her all at once, something Alex was not expecting. She shot out her energy burst, hitting one of them, knocking into another. She swung, hitting one across the face, stunning it enough for her to kick the next one closest to her. She took the arm of that one and swung it into the next closest one. Another infiltrator swiped, cutting her on the shoulder. Alex cringed and turned around to attack that one, but another grabbed her. She kicked one in the mouth, knocking it over, stunned. The one holding her threw her to the wall. She took a moment to catch her breath. She knew if Komptin didn't get up here soon, she wasn't going to last long. She ran to attack again but an infiltrator surprised her as she was forcefully pushed back into the wall. She dropped to the ground with drywall falling on top of her. The infiltrators gathered in a small circle around her, closing in. She knew this was going to be the end. She lit her fists, "Which one of you ugly asses are going to come with me?"

All of a sudden, a light burst came from across the room. It was strong enough to knock down three of the infiltrators. Alex didn't have time to question it. She took the one closest to her and began an offensive attack. The other one was preoccupied with a man she thought she was saving as his fists were lit as well. Alex couldn't believe another Lite Sentry was here and had not been told by the Council. She felt the infiltrator weaken and she jumped on its back. She formed a dagger and jabbed into the top of its head. It screamed in pain as it disappeared. Alex was still on top of it and she fell to the ground, landing on her backside. "Ow," she said, rubbing her butt. She quickly got up and realized two of the other Infiltrators were disappearing into the air as he was working on a third. "Holy shit!" Alex said. She knew there was another in the room although she didn't know where.

She decided to help the strange man who was breaking down the infiltrator. Alex ran up to the fight and finished it off by jabbing a generated knife into the back of it, coming out its chest. It screamed as it dropped and disappeared into the air. The two of them stood back-to-back, waiting for the next attack. They looked around the room.

"Seems the other has taken off," the man said. He dissipated the light and turned around to Alex. "My name is Sanah."

"Alex," she said, turning off her light as well. The two of them just stared at each other before Alex said, "I just have to ask, who the hell are you?"

"I'm a Lite Sentry, just as yourself," Sanah informed her. "My mission had led me here." Sanah examined the pale faced girl who only came up to his shoulders, and he wasn't the biggest guy on the planet. "What are you doing here?"

"College," Alex said, still staring at another Lite Sentry.

A scream of an infiltrator meeting its death echoed down the hall. "Is there another Lite Sentry here as well?" Sanah asked, paying attention to the direction of the noise.

"Well, not exactly," Alex said. Wall pieces went flying towards Sanah and Alex as Komptin stayed in the center of hole. "Hey, boy." Komptin walked up to Alex and rubbed his head across her body. "I'm okay, how about you?" She checked a scratch he had gotten on his side.

Sanah shook his head in disbelief. "Where did he come from?"

"He was kind of orphaned to me I guess you could say," Alex looked at her watch and then pulled out her phone. There were a lot of messages from Gastrix, no doubt upset that she wasn't at the club yet. "Oh, damn it, I'm late." She made her way out to the door. She looked back at Sanah. "Are you okay?"

"I'm good," Sanah replied out of shock that she was leaving.

"Let's meet up tomorrow for lunch," she offered. "I would love to talk to you."

Sanah agreed. "Sounds good."

Alex took off down the hallway and then came back into the room. "Here is my cell number. It was great to meet you! I can't believe I met another Lite Sentry."

* * *

Sanah waved good-bye to the girl he just met. It seemed to him there wasn't a lot to her. He wasn't too impressed. She was spunky, she had a big creature as her counterpart, but it seemed to him that she didn't take her duties too seriously. He didn't know what could be more important than the hunt. He just shook his head to chalk it up to youth, although as he recalled, he was much younger than she was when he was tasked. And then he took it seriously, really seriously. He looked at his watch. It was only a little after eleven at night. There were still hours of hunt left in the night. He thought he would just go ahead and start on another hunt.

There were more out there, and they had to be dealt with.

***

Salamor watched in the shadows as the two Lite Sentries destroyed his infiltrators. He examined the difference between the two. The Lite Sentry he had seen before was young, inexperienced, but she was headstrong, full of conviction and heart. Sanah on the other hand was different. Salamor could smell it a mile away. He was strong, really strong, with matching experience. But Salamor knew—he knew what he was going to do. Something that could tip the scale for the Dark to reign over this world.

Chapter 5

Alex rushed to dance to the club where Gastrix was anxiously waiting for her. She looked around the crowd for him. The dance club was busy, especially for a Sunday. She scouted around trying to find him. She saw the two girls from last night's club. They were enjoying the music as they danced together. This time they were wearing a white matching outfit. She continued to look around and felt a grip on her shoulder. She controlled herself from lighting up and turned to see Gastrix standing there.

"You're late," he said angrily as he stared her down.

"Sorry," Alex replied. "But things got out of hand at work."

"I thought you went for a walk?" he asked. "Don't lie to me!"

Alex quickly recovered, "I did, but then the church called me with an emergency."

Gastrix gave her a disgusting look of disappointment, "You're telling me you work for a church?" He just shook his head in disbelief. "You believe in that crap? Well, if you are that weak minded to fall for their propaganda." He took a sip of his drink. "You should have texted me. You made me look like an idiot in front of my friends. Not a good way to make a first impression."

Alex felt bad, "I'm sorry." She grabbed him by the shirt and pulled him in for a kiss. "I can make it up to you tonight."

"Damn right you will," he grinned. "Come on, let's go get crazy," he said, dragging Alex to the dance floor.

***

Mole couldn't stand it anymore. He was getting overanxious to try to do something to make him sweat. He got up early in his dorm room; he made sure not to wake Kameron up. He snuck out of the room where he ran into that girl again sneaking out of a different room.

"People are going to talk," Mole said to her as he yawned, heading to the bathroom.

She grazed his arm with her fingers, "We have to get caught first." She seductively smiled at him as she walked by.

A sudden rush of guilt came over him. He quickly rechecked himself to make sure he didn't disrespect Anne like that again. After his shower he put on his running shoes which he hadn't worn for quite a while. They felt good; it was like a part of him had been missing. He stepped down on the shoes and it felt as if he was walking on air. It was a feeling he never wanted to let go.

He got to the school gym and jumped on the treadmill. He closed his eyes. "Please let this feel good." He started off with a slow walk for about fifteen minutes and he didn't have any pain. He sped up the belt a little bit and could feel a small twinge in his back. He thought maybe it was just from being tight, so he continued to run through the pain. It seemed to subside as he warmed up his body. Now he was starting to feel good. He thought he would speed it up just a bit to get his heart racing. He was feeling good. He was going pretty well for about twenty minutes until his right leg began to feel a little funny. He thought he just landed on it wrong until he felt a tingling go from his back down to his leg. Then, the only thing he felt was his body crashing to the moving mat of the treadmill, carrying him to the bottom of the gym floor.

He laid for what seemed like an eternity until someone came running up to him. "Dude, you okay?" the big man asked. He extended his hand to offer help. Mole grabbed his hand and tried to get up but screamed in pain. The man turned to the guy next to him, "I think he's really hurt."

***

Anne just finished her morning class when she got the missed phone call from a number she didn't recognize. She played back the message where she heard the nurse tell her that Kale was in the emergency room. She ran to her car and tried to get a hold of Alex. The phone rang and rang but she didn't pick up. Anne frantically called Kale's mother who was just waking up.

"Ms. Moler, it's Anne," she said to her. "I just got a call that Kale is in the emergency room. I don't know what happened."

"What?" she said obviously awake now. "Do you know anything?"

"No, just that he was in the ER about a couple of hours ago," she said, feeling guilty. "I was in class; I had my phone on silent…"

"Honey, don't beat yourself up," she comforted her. "Just calm down, get to the hospital. I will call the hospital while you safely drive there. What hospital is it?"

Anne took a deep breath, "St. Peters."

"You just make sure you get there safe. He'll be okay."

"Okay," Anne said. She noticed that Alex was trying to call her back. "I gotta go, Alex is on the other line."

Anne switched over and answered the call, "Hey Alex,"

"What's going on?" Alex asked in a whisper.

"I can barely hear you," Anne said. She could hear some muffled complaining.

"Sorry, let me get into the other room," Alex replied. "What's up?"

"Mole is in the ER at St. Peters," Anne informed her. "I don't know what's going on."

"Okay, I will meet you there," she said, hanging up the phone.

Anne got to the check-in station at the hospital, "I'm here to see my boyfriend," Anne said. "I don't know where he is."

"Name?" the girl asked.

"Kale Moler," Anne said and then spelled his last name.

"Oh, here it is," she said, looking at the computer. "He was taken to Room 424." The girl handed her a visitor badge.

"Thank you," Anne said, grabbing the badge.

"Elevators are to the right, and it will be to your left down the hall."

"Thank you again," Anne said. She got into the elevator and texted Alex and Kale's mom the information on where he was.

She got down to the room where the door was partially open. She saw Kale in the hospital bed with a bandage on his head. She ran up to him and hugged him. "Honey, what happened?"

Kale found some courage to tell her the truth, "I tried running on the treadmill, something went wrong, and I crashed. I think I hit my head on the equipment," he said, grabbing his head.

"Yah you went down pretty hard," Kameron said, bringing in some water.

"Kameron," Anne said, "What are you doing here?"

"I was in the gym when the ambulance came and I saw Kale being hauled away," he informed her. "So, I thought I should see if he was okay until you got here."

"Thank you," Anne said as she moved Kale's hair away from his eyes.

"Yah, thanks," Kale said to his roommate. "You didn't have to stay, but I really appreciate it."

"No big," Kameron said, looking at his watch. "I'm going to go get some lunch. Do you want anything?"

"No, I'm good," Kale tried adjusting himself.

"Anne?"

"No thank you."

"Okay," Kameron said. He grabbed his wallet on the way out the door.

"What were you thinking?" Anne asked, giving him another hug.

"Not really in the mood for a lecture," Kale returned.

Anne pulled back from the hug, "Sorry, I just…never mind."

"It's okay. I'm sorry; I get it," he said, holding her hand.

The doctor came into the room. "Well, we had an interesting morning, didn't we?"

"You could say that," Kale responded.

"How are you feeling?" he asked Kale while shining a light in his eyes.

"I have a splitting headache," Kale said, grabbing his head.

The doctor looked to the nurse, ordering some pain medication. "Well, I understand you had an incident a couple of years back that caused you some reconstructive surgery on your back and knees."

"If you call getting the crap kicked out of you for no reason an 'incident'…" Kale responded.

"Kale," Anne quietly corrected him.

"Sorry, doc, long morning," he apologized.

"If that is the worst thing that happens to me today, then I'm going to have a good day," he assured him. "Well, a colleague of mine conferred along with our lead surgeon about your x-rays."

Anne could feel Kale start to tense as if he knew what was going to be said.

"The good news is, we can fix the spinal cord that is pressing on the nerve. It is an extremely low-key procedure" he said. "So, you don't have to worry; you will still be able to walk."

"Why do I feel there is a big 'but' coming?" Kale said, preparing for the news.

"I'm afraid you will never run again," he said. "In fact, people with this type of injury will be in pain from walking or standing or anything like that for an extended period of time."

Anne saw Kale fight back tears but he couldn't hold them in. She tried covering it up by hugging him. With her help he felt like he maintained his composure.

"I'm sorry," the doctor said. "I will come back and check in on you in a couple of hours." He put his hand on Kale's shoulder and gave him a comforting smile before he walked out of the room.

Anne sat with Kale for an hour before Alex came into the room. "I'm sorry I'm late," She ran over and gave Anne a hug. "What happened?" she whispered as she saw Kale sleeping.

Anne motioned to Alex that she wanted to talk outside, "He tried running and something happened with his nerve and spinal cord." Anne tried to explain, "Somehow they collided or something like that and he crashed onto the treadmill, hitting his head. Doctor said he will have to have a small procedure to repair the damage. He will be able to walk but he will never run again." Anne fought back tears. "I've never seen him so emotionally distraught,"

"He'll be okay," Alex said rubbing her arm. "He's strong."

Anne looked down at Anne's side, "Where's Komptin?"

"He's in the car," Alex said. "I forgot his Service Animal vest so I couldn't bring him in." Alex looked to the elevator. "Besides, I don't think Gastrix and Komptin get a long all that well."

The elevator opened and Gastrix came out alternately eating a sandwich and drinking a bottle of water. Anne turned around and went inside to check on Kale. Alex and her boyfriend walked into the room.

"What happened to him?" Gastrix loudly asked.

Kale tossed and turned and opened his eyes to the sight of Gastrix chomping away on a mouthful of food. He gave him a dirty look and turned to Anne. He rolled his eyes at her and she caught herself laughing. Alex walked up to Kale and gave him a hug. "You okay?"

Kale nodded his head, "Yah, I'm okay."

Alex stood up smiling at her brother. "Okay," she patted him on the arm and looked to Anne who had a look of worry on her face.

Gastrix was the first to break the silence, "I gotta get going. I'm meeting some people to mix this new beat I've been working on." He pointed to his watch.

"Can I go to the bathroom first?" Alex sarcastically asked.

Gastrix was annoyed but gave her permission. "Just hurry."

"Oh jeez, thank you," Alex said, walking past him.

Anne came closer to Kale who was trying to sit up. "Easy, honey," she did her best to help him adjust in the bed.

Anne and Kale both looked to the door where Kameron came in. "Oh, I'm sorry, I didn't know you had a visitor."

Kale said, "No, it came with Alex."

Anne looked at her watch, "I thought you left an hour ago."

"I was getting lunch when I got an important phone call," Kameron stated. "So, I just stayed in the cafeteria until it was over." Kameron put out his hand to shake Gastrix's, "Kameron."

Gastrix reluctantly shook his hand, "And you are?"

"I'm Kale's roommate," Kameron informed him. He turned his attention to Anne and Kale. "I'm sorry but I have an appointment I need to get to." Kameron gave Anne and Kale a brown paper bag. "I thought you two might be hungry, so I bought a couple of things from the cafeteria. There's some magazines in there as well in case you get bored."

"Thanks," Kale said, looking through the bag.

"Thank you," Anne said. She sat on the foot of Kale's bed and pulled out an apple.

"Let me know if you need anything from the dorm," Kameron said. He looked at his watch. "I really need to get going. Take care." He turned to Gastrix, "It was nice meeting you."

"Later," Gastrix said not giving him any consideration.

Kameron left the room and Gastrix looked to Kale and Anne. "Is he part of our little group here?"

Kale looked to Anne as if asking her to get him out of his room. Alex came into the room, drinking a bottle of water, "Are you ready to go?" she asked Gastrix.

"Yah, you better get me there in time," he said to her.

She walked over and gave Kale a kiss on the head and then hugged Anne. "I'll call you guys later." Kale and Anne just looked at each other in disbelief.

***

Alex was late to lunch with Sanah. She had found him eating a boneless chicken with rice and vegetables.

He stood up, "I was afraid you weren't going to make it."

"Yah, sorry I'm late," Alex said, looking at the menu. "My brother got hurt and had to go to the hospital."

"Is he, all right?" Sanah asked, "Was it an infiltrator attack?"

"No, not this time," Alex said. "But I think it was from when he was attacked."

"I'm sorry he was attacked. It's amazing he survived," Sanah said. "Most attacks on non-Sentries do not end well."

Alex remembered Sara's body lying on the couch in her house. "Yes, well, I did lose a sister that same night."

"I'm sorry," Sanah said. "But that is why we fight. This war cannot last forever."

"Do you know how long it has been going?" Alex inquired.

"Since man became aware of good and evil," Sanah answered.

"So, a couple of years now," Alex put down the menu. "I've been drinking water all day and I'm dying for an energy drink." She motioned for the

90

server and he came with a pitcher of water. "No water, please. Can I get three energy drinks?"

Sanah asked after the waiter left, "Do you still sleep?"

"No," Alex said. "I just like the taste of them." Alex put some water in a bowl and gave it to Komptin who was sleeping next to her feet. "Sometimes I think he sleeps just to show off."

"Where did he come from?" Sanah asked, looking at him. "He's massive even in that state."

Alex chuckled, "He was my former mentor's. He died saving myself and someone very important to us."

"I'm sorry, was he a Sentry?"

Alex shook her head no. "Not exactly. Let's just say he had extensive knowledge of us from both perspectives."

"He was Dark Sentry?" Sanah dropped back in his chair.

"I can honestly say he was nowhere near the Dark," Alex reassured him. "He was a good man." She looked up to the sky where she saw the faint purple star. "We really miss him at times." She petted Komptin on the head.

"I will say a peace prayer tonight for you all," Sanah offered to her.

"Thank you," The waiter came over and gave her the drinks she ordered. As he left he gave her a quick little wink and smile. Alex smiled back, "You know before I had a boyfriend, I probably would have made his night."

Sanah looked up at the guy walking away. "So where did the dog come in?"

"He was a protector assigned to Osiah," Alex said.

"Osiah?" Sanah again dropped back in his chair. "You are telling me your trainer was Osiah? From the Dark?"

"Yah, why?" Alex said, drinking her energy drink. "Do you know him?"

"Just stories and myths," Sanah explained. "Legend has it that he fell in love with the Conduit and instantly turned on the Dark. He and..." Sanah was thinking back for a name. "Vandle, I think his name was, were feared when they approached the Angels of Lite in battle."

"Vandle?" Alex asked. "Oh, you mean Vandor?"

"Yes, that's it."

"He is a black-hearted bastard, let me tell you," Alex pointed to a double cheeseburger on the menu. "I gotta eat this quick."

"You've come across him... and survived?" Sanah asked, trying to get the conversation back to Vandor.

Alex felt a little embarrassed telling this story, "Not really, we've crossed paths a couple of times. I tried fighting him once, but he overpowered me instantly." She thought back about that night. "He actually just wanted to talk... weird. I guess I never really thought about that." Alex shrugged it off. "Oh well. Do you have a trainer?"

"Long ago. He was another Lite Sentry sent to me by the Islamic Council. He passed away about five years ago," Sanah informed her.

"I'm sorry," Alex said. "Did he die by infiltrators?"

Sanah laughed, "No. He was ninety-three years old."

"Oh," Alex smiled. She looked at her phone as a text came in from Gastrix telling her that he needed to be picked up in an hour. Alex texted back that she was at lunch with a friend. He replied back with his order for food.

"Are you ready to order?" the waiter asked.

"Yes, I will have a double bacon cheeseburger, a side of fries, and a combination platter as an appetizer," Alex said. "And then a boneless chicken pita to go when you bring the check."

"Hungry?" Sanah asked.

"My boyfriend wants me to bring him lunch," Alex said. "Do you have anybody?"

Sanah patted the letter he wrote to his wife and kid. "I was just mailing my letter to my wife and son today actually."

Alex smiled as she knew she could never have kids, "That's sweet."

Sanah returned the smile. "They are everything to me."

***

Salamor enjoyed trolling the hospitals. It wasn't the physical pain he relished, it was more the giving up on life he desired. There were certain floors of this massive building that were full of despair compared to some other structures he visited.

He enjoyed the bald adults hooked to the tubes the best. The constant pain and sickness they were in combined with the teetering of death made for a

93

pleasurable atmosphere. He took pleasure in toying with their emotions to the point of telling them to give up all hope and watch them die from pure lack of will to live.

Salamor jumped from shadow to shadow, hiding in the darkness of the building. He overheard laughter coming from one room. It made him sick to hear such joy from a building of sorrow. He wanted to avoid the room altogether but something familiar caught his attention. He knew that feeling and he needed to confirm it. He peeked into the room to see a boy and a girl sitting on the bed laughing.

This room had something special to it. Salamor stayed in the shadows to take the feeling in. The boy was lying to the one he loved. He was falsely showing happiness but deep down he was falling quickly. Salamor salivated at the treachery. With a little work, he could bring him to the point of death. But there was something else, the girl he was holding hands with! His excitement overtook him. Salamor wanted to approach her and confirm, but he would have to wait as a familiar sound was in the room.

He heard that sound again. He jumped into the darkness of the shadows and saw the Lite Sentry with her creature at her side on the other side of the bed. The creature lifted his head up and growled while flashing his eyes. "Komptin," the Sentry said. "Not here." The Sentry got up from the chair.

"What is it?" the boy asked while flipping through the glowing box on the wall.

"Nothing," the Sentry said. She got up and looked out the window and then walked past Salamor to see if anything was out in the hallway.

Komptin stared to the dark where Salamor was hiding, with a fierce look to his eyes. Salamor decided it was time to exit the building.

***

"That was weird," Alex said, coming back into the room. She opened the door to the patient's bathroom to see what was going on.

"What are you looking for?" Anne asked.

"Nothing to worry about," Alex said motioning to Komptin who was now sniffing around the room. Alex clicked the leash on him. "I'm going to take Komptin on a walk."

Anne immediately turned her attention to Alex.

Alex just mouthed, "It's fine." She put her hand up to Anne to tell her not to worry and to stay put.

Anne gave her a smile as she snuggled close to Mole who was trying to find something on the television.

"I gotta go, I will talk to you tomorrow," Alex told Mole.

"I'm getting discharged tomorrow," he told her.

"He'll be staying with us for a week," Anne said. "I got to take care of my man."

Mole smiled and kissed her on the forehead.

"Okay, sounds good. Come on, Komptin," Alex said as they walked out of the hospital.

***

Sanah got a text from Alex about a hunt of a creature that hid in the shadows that she initiated. He had heard of such a creature, but he had never come across one before. He has read that they couldn't be destroyed. They liked to prey on the ones who have given up on life. He didn't understand why this new Sentry has had more experience with various versions of the Dark while he only dealt with infiltrators and the occasional demon or host.

He cleaned up after his evening prayer and gathered a small bag of food for the young girl in his apartment. He picked up a couple of candy bars from the gas station on his way home and also put in a few nutritional items. He thought now would be a good time to finish his letter to his wife.

My Dear,

I had found some good news in my fight against the Dark. I came across another Lite Sentry. She is young, inexperienced, but she has potential. I don't understand why the Lite doesn't activate more. Perhaps the Lite wants to keep this secret war hidden from the public view. I really wished they wouldn't. I'm getting tired. I wanna come home.

I love you always.

Sanah went to mail his letter in the post office across town. On the way he delivered the bag of food he put together to the young girl who smiled in return. He smiled back at her and went onto his hunt with the young lady who was entrusted as a Lite Sentry. They decided to meet at an old hospital that had been abandoned for some time now. The feeling of negative dark air filled the room as he could imagine all the sick and elderly people that had once filled it. He walked around quietly as he heard some commotion up near one of the hallways. He made sure not to make any noise. It was dark, but he welcomed it because he could hide from the infiltrators before an attack. More noise came from the end of the hallway in a room. Sanah leaned his head around the corner to see Alex balancing an old wheelchair on two wheels. Sanah must have startled her because she fell on her back.

"Oh hey," she said to him, quickly picking herself off the floor. "Didn't hear you coming."

Sanah could feel himself getting irritated with her lack of commitment to the hunt. He almost viewed her as a young child who was thinking this was a game. He believed she didn't understand the weight of responsibility she was entrusted with. "I caught a sense of an infiltrator here. I do not have any knowledge of this shadow creature you have seen."

The young girl walked towards the door, veering into the hallway. "All I know about him is that he was a little minion of Vandor." She looked back at Sanah. "And he cannot be killed."

"You mean he's strong and powerful?" Sanah inquired.

"No, meaning there is nothing to him. He is not physical; he's just dark air, a living shadow."

"So, what's so dangerous about him?"

Alex turned around to face Sanah. "He preys on the weak minded," she told him. In an instant Alex screamed as she was grabbed from behind and thrown into the room across the hall. An infiltrator had snuck up on all three of them. Komptin morphed into his fighting form and crashed through the wall to quickly get to Alex.

Sanah lit his fists and entered the room where two infiltrators came in from the fire escape. Two more infiltrators were running away down the hallway. "Go on, I got this," Alex said to Sanah. She activated her powers and attacked the two killers.

Sanah ran down the hallway into the darkness where the infiltrators were last seen. He picked up their trails leading downstairs on the next floor. It was dark, it was quiet. Sanah could hear Alex's battle above him. There was a different feeling in the air. All he knew was that it was Dark.

"Give up,"

Sanah turned around quickly to see who was behind him. He lifted his hands to see if there was anyone around. He turned back to the hunt.

"The Lite is dim."

Sanah turned around again. He saw nothing. He looked out the window where the infiltrators must have escaped from his hunt. He was mad at himself. He hardly ever let infiltrators get the drop on him let alone escape from his hunt.

"The next generation doesn't care."

He turned around again to see where that voice was coming from. He heard Alex screaming at the infiltrator from above him. He assumed she won the battle because she was bragging on her skills to the dead creature as it disappeared.

Alex met him downstairs where he was looking out the window. "There's two more on the run." He turned to look at her as she looked at her phone. "We should go after them."

She looked at him with disgust. "Can you get it? I have to go take care of something personal."

"I guess," Sanah said, turning around, looking out the window.

"Thanks, I owe you," Alex said, heading out the door.

Komptin looked back and forth to the window as Alex left. Sanah thought he could actually see disappointment in the creature's face as he morphed back to being a dog. Komptin slowly turned to Alex's direction as he headed out the door.

"She doesn't care."

"No, she doesn't," Sanah agreed to the voice behind him.

***

Alex got to the bar where Gastrix was talking to a bunch of people about the mix he put together earlier. "Hey sorry I'm late." She grabbed his hand. He pulled away and gave her a dirty look. "What's wrong?"

Gastrix walked over to the other side of the bar and Alex followed him. "What the hell?!"

"What?" Alex asked him in defense.

"You said you were going to come here right after visiting your brother from the hospital," Gastrix pointed out, taking in a drink. "You made me look like an idiot in front of our friends."

Alex turned around to the group. "I don't know these people."

"Which makes it worse; the first impression to our friends meeting you and you don't show up on time. Ridiculous," he shook his head. "Where did you go anyways?"

"I took Komptin for his walk," Alex replied.

"For that long? This late at night?" Gastrix inquired. "Is there some other guy or something?"

Alex smiled as she grabbed his red leather cut off sleeve jacket. "No, of course not." She kissed him. "I'm a one-man woman."

Gastrix rolled his eyes as he finished his drink. "You better be. Do not to make me look like an idiot again."

"I'm sorry," Alex said. "Let me buy you a drink."

"You should buy a round for our friends to show you're sorry," he told her.

Alex looked at her wallet. She knew the church was going to question such a high credit card bill. They didn't mind her being a kid, but they were pretty sincere about not taking advantage of their arrangement. She thought she might be able to cover it. "Okay," she reluctantly agreed.

Alex came up to the bar. "A round for my friends over there," Alex said. She felt awkward saying that. She sat down at the bar waiting for the drinks to be made when she was approached by two girls holding hands together were dressed in the same outfit as each other, this time in neon orange. "Hi. Didn't I see you a couple of weeks ago at Distance?"

"Yes, you did," the one on the left said to Alex.

"She's cute," the other said.

"Yes, she is. I'm Shelly," she said.

"I'm Tory."

Alex extended her hand, the two of them caught her off guard and gave her a hug. "Oh, okay." Alex hugged back.

Gastrix walked over to Alex. "Where are those drinks?" He looked over at Shelly and Tory. "Shell, Tore."

"Gastrix," the two of them said together.

Alex smirked.

"What's so funny?" Gastrix asked her.

"They just reminded me of two others I know," Alex said. She started to gather the drinks together to bring to her new 'friends' whom she never met.

"How come I never met them?" Gastrix asked her. "I thought I met all the people you hung out with."

Alex was trying to formulate her words, "They are not from around here; I rarely see them."

Gastrix replied, "More secrets." He waved her off. "Whatever." He walked off, irritated.

Alex went to follow him when she was grabbed by one of the girls. "If there is anything you need to talk about, you can call any of us."

The other girl pulled a business card out of her bra and handed it to Alex who read it out loud. "Chix Fiber Fix?" Alex looked at them in confusion. "Computer repair."

"Yes, but if there is anything else you may need, call us."

Alex put it in her purse. "Thanks." She started walking off. "It was nice meeting you."

"Likewise," the two of them said together. They watched Alex join Gastrix with his friends. The two of them just shared a worried look.

Chapter 6

Sanah was on his way home after the hunt. He had caught up to the two infiltrators with relative ease. The encounter was brief, and he extinguished their existence on this planet, but one of them got a slice of his arm before it was dissipated. He passed a couple of elderly men who had been sleeping on a bench nuzzled together under a blanket, trying to keep warm. He put his head down in shame as he had trouble seeing his fellow man in such misery.

"Useless to fight."

Sanah heard that voice again as he turned around quickly to see where it was coming from. A prostitute met eyes with Sanah as she approached him. "Hey baby, you looking for a morning quickie?"

"No, thank you," Sanah replied, trying to get to his apartment.

"Come on, honey," she walked up to him. She grabbed his hand. Sanah looked down and saw the remnants of drug track marks on her arms.

"I must go," Sanah pulled his hand away from her grasp. He walked away and a big man approached the girl, telling her that she needed to earn her keep. He grabbed her and kicked her butt, degrading her. She screamed as she was forced inside the building where she was standing.

"They are not worth it."

Sanah looked towards the peak of the Mosque as it peeked over the buildings in the morning sun. "I need to pray."

***

Anne woke up to the sound of Alex and Gastrix yelling at each other. Anne tried covering her ears with her pillow, but it was useless. She looked at the time. It was early morning but too late in the morning to try to fall back asleep. She looked over at the emptiness of the other side of her bed. She missed waking up next to Kale.

Anne walked out of her bedroom where Brenda was eating her breakfast on the couch, watching cartoons. "They have been at it for, like, forever already," she informed her.

"What about?" Anne said, looking down the hall at Alex's room.

"I don't know. Something about her not caring about him because of something self-centered she did last night," Brenda informed her.

"Alex...self-centered?" Anne just shook her head with disgust. She grabbed her phone and texted Kale. "Hope you had a good night's rest. I will be by at lunch. Let me know if you need something. Love you!" She was just about to hit send but she stopped herself and erased the "Love you." She realized the first time she said that to him shouldn't be in text messages.

Anne got a reply back, "Rough night. Back was hurting. Would love a real big burger. Missed you last night."

Anne blushed as she thought he must have been reading her mind. "Missed you, too," she replied.

"You okay?" Brenda asked.

"Fine, why?" Anne asked.

"You just got red."

Anne realized she really was blushing. Even after all these years, Kale made her feel like they did when they first started dating. That was broken up by the sound of Alex leaving her room. She waved to Anne. "Morning."

"Good morning," Anne said. She rubbed Alex's back as she walked past. "You okay, sweetie?"

"I'm fine," Alex sharply said. Komptin hopped off the chair and came to Alex's side. She rubbed his ears. "I'm sorry, boy."

Anne and Alex walked into the kitchen where Alex made organic egg whites and poured herself a non-concentrate orange juice. Anne watched her eat the eggs. "Eating healthy these days?"

"Gastrix doesn't like me eating unhealthy food. He said he doesn't want me to gain weight."

"So, what if you do?" Anne was surprised Alex was allowing someone to influence her like that.

"He's just looking out for my well-being," Alex told her. "Let's face it. I really don't eat the healthiest."

"I'm all for you eating healthy if you want to do it, but just make sure it is for the right reason," Anne tried to remind her.

"What's that supposed mean?" Alex snapped back.

Anne put up her hands, "Hey, I didn't mean anything by it. I'm sorry if I upset you."

"It's okay," Alex tried to calm herself down. "Is Mole going to get out of the hospital in time for his birthday party?"

"Remember he gets released today?" Anne said. "I will bring him here for a couple of days before he goes back to school."

Alex tried to remember, "Oh yah, is the dinner ready for Saturday?"

Anne nodded as she sipped her coffee.

"Who's going to the dinner?"

"Well, so far I got you, me, Dan, Brenda, Kale's mom, and Kameron," Anne told her.

"Who's Kameron?" Alex asked, trying to force down her egg whites.

"Kale's roommate. He stayed with Kale at the hospital until I got there," Anne said. "They never really talked much but I thought I would invite him as kind of a thank you."

"Sounds like a fun evening. Don't forget Gastrix," Alex pointed out.

Anne lied through her teeth in hopes of showing support for her friend, "Yes, I counted him with your reservation."

Alex smiled, "Thank you."

***

Mole just got done with talking to the doctor. He picked up the TV remote and started flipping through the channels where they were televising an Iron Man competition. He started watching when he caught himself missing it.

"Never again."

Mole quickly turned the channel where a beer commercial came on. Mole stepped back and remembered how carefree he used to feel when he drank.

106

"You can have that feeling again."

Mole shut the TV off again and started going through Facebook on his phone. He came across a photo of himself and Joseph on their bikes with their arms around each other.

"You're all alone."

Mole shut the phone off as the nurse came in. "Is everything all right, Mr. Moler?"

"I'm just a little bit more sore than usual; can I get something to ease the pain?"

"Let me see what I can do," the nurse replied.

***

Sanah left the mosque after morning prayers. Usually when he was feeling this down and out, a prayer session recharged him in a way, but not today. He stepped outside of the mosque where a lady pulled her young child away from him. He overheard her tell him that the mosque is where terrorists are bred. There was so much ignorance and hate in the world.

Sanah walked into the gas station where the young teenager behind the counter was reading a pamphlet with an upside four on it. "So right, man," the young male said.

Sanah gathered up some food and stopped at the ATM to grab some cash. He needed to do some good in the world, so he pulled out 300 dollars. He placed the money in the bag and bought some groceries for the young girl and her mother.

He walked through the hallway and found the little girl playing with one of the toys which he bought for her. As he had done in the past, he just

107

placed the bag next to the girl without saying a word. The two just smiled at each other and he walked away, knowing he had done some good in the world.

***

Alex helped Anne carry Mole into the living room and gently place him on the couch. "You okay, honey?" Anne asked Mole as she set his leg on the pillow.

"I'm good," he said as he settled himself.

"Okay," Anne said, organizing her thoughts. "Dan talked to all your teachers for you, and they gathered all your homework in your email. Looks like they said you can finish up the classes via distance learning. Alex will stay here with you while I go pick up your prescriptions at the pharmacy and I will pick up something to eat for lunch." Anne looked at Alex in acknowledgement. "Anything else?"

"No, I'm good," Mole said.

"Okay," Anne sighed. She leaned in and kissed Mole.

Mole put his hand through Anne's hair and looked into her eyes. "Anne, I…I…just wanted to say…I couldn't have done this without you."

Anne smiled, "Of course, I would do anything for you,"

Mole gave her a dirty smirk.

"But I won't do that," Anne laughed at him as she playfully played with his hair.

"She Meatloaf'ed me!" Mole grinned. He playfully slapped her on her butt.

She laughed as she turned to Alex, "Do you need anything?"

Alex smiled at the two of them, "No, I'm good."

Anne got up and headed out the door. "Okay, just text me if you need or want anything."

Mole and Alex both gave her thumbs up.

"You guys are so cute together. She's got such a big heart to her," Alex told Mole who was logging into his laptop.

He was typing in his laptop and replied, "Yah, that's why I love her."

Alex spat out her Apollo drink. "What?" she said, wiping water from her mouth.

"What?" Kale said, peering over his laptop at her.

"You love her?" Alex asked.

Mole looked at her, "Come on, Alex. We've been dating since high school. She's the only girl I've been with and the only one I want to be with. She's smart, beautiful, patient, and so kindhearted. I think of her when I'm not with her, and she's the center of my focus when we are together." He opened an orange juice Anne placed for him. "If that's not love, then I'm not sure what is."

"Have you told her?" Alex asked, knowing the answer.

"Not yet. I'm trying, but what if she just doesn't feel the same?" Kale asked her.

"You're an idiot."

***

Mole was enjoying the alone time with Alex. They never really got to spend that much time together with just the two of them. Even though they were just watching TV. The sound from down the hallway caught Mole's attention. "Is Brenda here?"

Alex quickly chugged down her Apollo drink and placed the can underneath the chair. "Gastrix is getting up."

It took every ounce of strength for Mole not to roll his eyes. "Oh goody," he said, opening up one of his schoolbooks.

"Hey, honey," Alex said, running up to Gastrix.

"Hey. We need more toilet paper in our bathroom."

"Okay," Alex said, going into the closet and pulling out the toilet paper. "Here you go."

"Come on, I just got up. You go change it," Gastrix said, sitting down on the chair where Alex had been sitting. He grabbed the remote and put on some anime.

Mole looked at the TV because everything was in Japanese with American subtitles.

Alex returned back from dealing with the bathroom crisis of no toilet paper. She was looking at her phone. "I got a text from Anne saying that there is a problem with the prescription, and she can't get lunch. She asked if I could go get it."

"Please, take Gastrix, please, take Gastrix," Mole thought to himself.

"Okay, we are just sitting here watching anime anyways," Gastrix said to Alex. "Pick me up a couple of those little shooters of whiskey."

"Anything else?" Alex sarcastically asked.

"Stop the 'tude would be nice," Gastrix said. "Or do we need to have that discussion again?"

"Okay, I'm sorry," Alex quickly gave in. "I'll go get them."

Mole looked at Alex, "Don't you fricking leave me, Alex."

"You'll be fine, you big ape," Alex told him. She grabbed her keys. "Come on, Komptin." Komptin eagerly jumped off the couch and headed to the door.

Gastrix put his feet on the coffee table and turned up the volume on the TV. "I swear she likes that damn dog more than me."

Instantly Mole thought, "I like the dog more than you," but he refrained from saying it. All he said was, "She had that dog for a long time."

"Joy," Gastrix pulled out a joint and started lighting it up.

"Hey, dude, we're 420 free."

"Relax, man, expand your horizons," Gastrix told him.

"Alex's dad is a prosecuting attorney," he informed Gastrix. Mole tried to get back to his computer to log into his class.

"He wouldn't send his daughter's boyfriend to jail," Gastrix confidentially told him.

"He sent his own son to jail for four months, so take that what you will," Mole pointed out.

"Seriously?"

"Yep."

Gastrix put out his cigarette. "I'm going to bring out my laptop and lay down some new beats I've been thinking of."

Mole just closed his eyes, hoping Anne or Alex would get back soon.

***

Anne came home with Mole, just staring at Gastrix who was working on his music quite loudly. All Anne got was a look of "help me" when she walked through the door. "Alex isn't back yet?"

"Nope," Mole continued to type in his laptop. "Please tell me you have my drugs…you know, the ones that knock me out…. for a very long time."

Anne shook the bag. "Right here." Anne turned to Gastrix. "Do you mind if I talk to Kale?"

"No, go ahead," Gastrix said continuing to play the song he was working on.

"She meant alone," Mole said.

Gastrix rolled his eyes, "Whatever, man." He put his headphones on and plugged them into the computer.

"Do you think he can hear us?" Anne asked, staring at Kale.

"Gastrix, you're a piece of crap who treats Alex horribly and if you were half a man with a quarter of a brain you would realize that no one likes you," Mole said to him.

Gastrix continued to work on his music.

Mole looked over at him, "What does she see in him?"

"Honey," Anne said to Kale. "This is serious."

"Okay, what is it," Mole started to pay attention to Anne.

"I talked to the pharmacist," Anne told him. "She said that I need to be really strict with the dosage on them since you are a recovering alcoholic."

"Okay," Mole adjusted his position on the couch. He never enjoyed these conversations since it was embarrassing for him to talk about.

"I know what I want to do, but I want you to tell me what you think I should do in giving you these pills," Anne stated.

Mole knew he had to swallow his pride on this one, "Well, how about you completely hide them from me. Don't tell me where they are, or anyone, and just give them to me when necessary."

Anne placed her hands on the side of Kale's face and kissed him, "I love you, Kale Moler."

Mole reached over on the end table and grabbed a flower from the vase. He broke some of the stem and placed the flower in Anne's hair. "I love you, Anne McClure."

***

Sanah stared out the window facing the east. He could feel the sun beating on him from the other side of the apartment window. He realized that he had missed his prayer and just spent the time looking out the window.

"Humanity is failing"

He just stared out the window. He must be getting tired because those thoughts had been more constant. It also came to his attention that he hadn't written to his wife and son lately. He got up from the rug and left it by the window. He opened the fridge and pulled out his dinner. He didn't feel like eating.

113

"He doesn't care anymore."

Sanah shook his head and started to go out for his hunt for the night. He picked up his phone to text Alex to meet up for a hunt.

"Her priorities are not where they should be."

Sanah put away his phone. He knew that she didn't care. It was a thrill ride for her. She never understood the importance of choosing a side.

***

It was late when Alex and Gastrix left the bar. Gastrix was in a somewhat good mood. He put his arm around her neck as she walked down the street.

"Tonight, was fun," Alex said as she was trying to walk with him.

"Yeah, it was," Gastrix said. "But I think you should really start changing your outfits before coming out."

"You don't like the way I dress?" Alex said, looking at her outfit.

"You're too industrial," Gastrix told her.

"Excuse me?" Alex said, getting a tad bit upset. "Too industrial?"

"We are a cyber couple. I don't want to be embarrassed around our friends," he stated.

"I guess I can change some of my outfits," Alex said.

"You can remove your weave as well and get something a bit more cyber; neon red!" He played with her hair.

"Okay…" Alex felt like she got kicked in the gut by a weightlifting demon.

"And it's nice to walk without your dog following us everywhere," he continued to educate her. "It's not healthy to have that kind of attachment to an animal."

"Anything else?" she asked, almost afraid of the answer.

"No, you just work on that," he said. "But you know I love you, right?"

"You do," Alex smiled at him.

"Of course, you're hot! And if you dress correctly everyone will be jealous of what I have," Gastrix pointed out, drinking more of his alcohol shooters.

Alex smiled at the fact that he said she was his girlfriend and he cared so much for her. Alex was about to tell him that she loved him too, but something caught her attention. She stopped in the middle of the sidewalk. She looked behind her and down the street a bit.

"What's with you?"

"I think we need to turn around," Alex said. She looked down the darkened street. The sense of the Dark was about.

"Why?"

Alex thought of the first thing that would get him to turn around, "I'm scared."

"Don't worry, there's nothing to be afraid of," Gastrix said. They continued to walk down the dark street. Alex noticed that the lights were broken, making the street darker.

"Damn it, not again," Alex said out loud.

"What are you babbling about?" Gastrix asked.

"Nothing, we should really go. This part of town has high crime," Alex insisted. She turned around and caught a glimpse of some red eyes down the alley from their direction. "Damn it."

"Okay, you're starting to be a little annoying with this. Let's go, we're almost home."

Alex saw a figure appear out of the dark ahead of them. She was relieved to see Sanah come out of the shadows. "Oh, thank God."

"Alex," Sanah said in greeting her. "Are you...doing what I think you are doing with him?"

"Sanah, we are just coming back from the bar," Alex said nervously. "This is my boyfriend."

Gastrix pulled Alex in closer to him, "I'm Gastrix. Who are you?"

"I'm Sanah," he replied. He scanned the area around him to be sure no infiltrators were coming up behind them.

"How do you know Alex?" Gastrix grilled Sanah.

"We work together," Sanah said looking at Alex in disbelief. "In fact, we have some work that needs to be taken care of."

"I know," Alex said. "I recently came across it."

"We should take care of it."

Gastrix interrupted, "Dude, it can wait until tomorrow."

Alex could tell Sanah was getting annoyed. Sanah said, "Look, there is a church right over there. You could drop...Gas...twix over there and we can take care of it."

"Look Arab, my name is Gastrix," he said. "Alex, you go with him and you can forget about us...forever."

"Sanah," she looked back at the alley. "I gotta go."

"Really?" Sanah said in shock.

"I will catch up with you tomorrow," Alex said. "But I think I want to go home with Gastrix."

"Whatever. I will take care of it," Sanah started to walk away, but stopped himself to turn around. "You need to seriously look at yourself and set your priorities."

"Sanah," Alex said. "Wait."

"Get out of here, man," Gastrix yelled. "He really needs to get a girl."

"He's married with a son," Alex quietly told him.

"I bet his wife is porking the pizza delivery boy because he's out this late working," Gastrix said loudly so Sanah could hear him.

Alex cringed as soon as Gastrix said that. Next thing she saw was Sanah grabbing Gastrix and throwing him up against a brick wall of a building, holding Gastrix up off the ground. "SANAH! STOP IT!" Alex yelled.

Sanah moved his hands from Gastrix's jacket to his throat, choking him. "You don't have the right to speak about my wife and son."

"SANAH!" Alex screamed. She tried pulling his arm off Gastrix but it wouldn't budge.

Sanah pushed Alex with ease. Sanah regained his composure. "You are not worth it. You are not worth protecting." He turned to Alex. "And you, you are not even close to being worthy of what you got." He started to walk away from Alex, he turned to her. "Don't ever call for me again."

"Sanah," Alex cried to him. She turned her attention to Gastrix. "Are you okay?"

Gastrix got himself up and pushed Alex away from him. "Are you doing him too?!" He grabbed her by the arms and squeezed. If Alex didn't have the Lite in her, she thought that this would actually have been painful by human standards.

"No," Alex said. "We just work together."

Gastrix swung Alex around, throwing her into the same brick wall where he was once pinned. "I swear, bitch, if you are lying to me." He pointed his finger at her and slapped her across the face. Gastrix let go of her and walked off in a fit of rage.

Alex went running after him, pleading to come back. "Gastrix, wait."

***

Salamor came out of the shadows with the infiltrator at his side. "Almost there." He disappeared into the darkness.

***

Sanah had never been so mad before. He couldn't believe that He had entrusted such a self-centered little girl to such a responsible mission for humanity. He looked back at Alex and just saw her running after her boyfriend into the darkness. Sanah just bit his lip and turned back around to see a shadow figure with red eyes in front of him. Sanah ignited his fists and swung, passing through the figure's body.

"Sanah, I presume," the misty figured hissed.

"Yes," Sanah replied looking around. He knew there were infiltrators here, but he couldn't see any. That meant he wasn't going to get a surprise attack on him.

"Let me introduce myself. My master calls me Salamor," it informed him. He floated to a dumpster and sat on it looking at Sanah.

"I assume you want something," Sanah said. "You have nothing I want to hear."

"I need you to help me," Salamor asked of the Lite Sentry.

Sanah rolled his eyes, "Not happening," he turned around and started to walk away but Salamor appeared in front of him again.

"You will not be able to pass this up," Salamor got Sanah's attention. "I need help with my own conflict."

Sanah stopped, "What do you mean?"

"I'm torn. I don't understand this war. I need you to convince me that Lite is the side I should follow," Salamor said. "Think of all that I can do for you. Think about it. That Lite Sentry girl has that massive creature as her companion, think of what I could do for you."

Sanah stopped and looked to the stars. "She is so self-centered and doesn't care about this war. I don't understand why He would give her such power."

Salamor put his arm around Sanah. "She would rather spend time with an abusive male primate than help you fight this war." Salamor floated with Sanah as he started to walk. "The scars you have on your body, the losses you have witnessed through your battles, what have they gotten you? What is your reward?" Salamor pointed to humans on the other side of the street: a hooker, the homeless, drug dealers. "I just don't understand why you fight for them. You have a diseased hooker who knowingly spreads her disease to others that have sworn to God that they will spend their life with their mate. You have this guy over here who sells harmful chemicals to little children for currency. I just don't know what Lite does for humanity. Why do you fight for them? Tell Salamor why, so I can understand."

Sanah broke free from Salamor's grasp. "There is good. If I do good, then others will thrive from my sacrifice."

Salamor approached him from the back and whispered in his ear, "I just don't know if I should defect from the Dark if this is what the Lite has to offer."

Sanah turned around to find that Salamor had left into the darkness of the alley.

***

Anne was in deep relaxation. She was on the couch with Kale in complete happiness. She was sitting up on one end of the couch, Kale was on the other. She was drinking a glass of wine while he was having some apple juice. The lights were low and soft music was playing in the background. Anne looked over at the man she loved and smiled. He smiled back at her. Komptin was lying on the chair next to Anne.

Anne felt safe. Not just because she had Alex's massive gargoyle creature lying in the chair on the other side of the room, but emotionally safe. She noticed Komptin's ears perk and his body grew tense. Kale noticed it as well as he stopped massaging Anne's feet. Kale looked to the door where Komptin was staring and giving a low growl.

The door swung open and Gastrix walked in as if he owned the place. "I don't want to hear it!"

Alex came in after him, "Listen to me."

Gastrix turned around and pointed his finger at her, "One, you don't ever tell me what to do. Two, how can I trust you if you were out with that guy 'working'," he air-quoted. "Slut," he called her as he went to walk back to the bedroom.

"I should have told you, I'm sorry," Alex pleaded.

Anne and Kale would have left for the bedroom, but Kale was still laid up on the couch. The two of them just looked at each other confused.

"Do you know how bad you treat me?" Gastrix asked her. "How much you hurt me?"

Anne choked on her wine.

Alex had just realized that she had an audience. "You don't have to act so angry about this."

Gastrix forcefully walked up to her and raised his hand, "Act? I'm far from acting."

Alex didn't budge; all she did was put her finger in the air towards Komptin, telling him not to attack. Anne turned to Komptin whose eyes were glowing blue. Luckily, Kale was paying attention to Gastrix. Alex turned her face to Komptin and snapped her fingers, pointing down at the chair. Komptin reluctantly laid back down, keeping his attention on Gastrix.

Gastrix looked at the dog. He put his hand down. "I'm not your dog to command at will." He walked off into the bedroom, slamming the door, breaking a picture off the wall.

Alex closed her eyes and took a deep breath. She regained her composure and joined Komptin on the chair. Komptin put his head on Alex's lap. "It's okay, boy."

Anne, along with Kale, looked at Alex. Alex shamefully looked back at them. For what seemed like an eternity no one said anything until Kale broke the silence, "So, how was your night?"

***

Sanah was on his way home when he noticed the lights outside his apartment. He saw a police officer standing next to the door in the hallway where the little girl and her mother resided. He peeked through the door to see the little girl with a needle in her arm, lying on the ground, motionless. The mother was obviously in some sort of narcotic state.

He approached the officer. "What happened?"

"Do you know the two?" the officer asked him.

Sanah shook his head no. "I just know they lived in the apartment. I give them food and money on occasion."

Sanah just stared at the lifeless child on the ground with the mom handcuffed, sitting on the couch. He knew he should feel sorrow but was overcome with anger.

The officer said, "As far as I could tell, the mom was shooting up and what we could get out of her, the daughter grabbed an extra needle from her mom's stash and overdosed. Shameful."

Sanah noticed the bag that he put the money in. He knew then the money was used to purchase the drugs that killed the little girl. Sanah moved away as the police officer asked him to step back for the ambulance attendants to take the body. Sanah made it back to the apartment, looking out the window over the park. He rolled his prayer rug and threw it in the garbage. He felt Salamor enter the apartment.

Salamor didn't get to speak before Sanah said, "I have one condition. I am not to be infiltrated."

"As you wish," Salamor said, backing off into a corner.

Sanah's eyes flashed purple as he watched the ambulance take the little girl's body away.

Chapter 7

Mole woke up in the morning with Anne fast asleep next to him. He thought he would get started on his homework before heading to his physical therapist. He carefully got out of bed, hopping over to his cane. He limped to the dresser where he had put the laptop but couldn't find it. He looked and saw it on the floor where it must have dropped when Gastrix slammed the door to Alex's bedroom. He picked it up off the floor, hoping it still worked and carried it into the kitchen where Alex was eating her egg-white omelet. "Couldn't sleep?" he asked her.

Alex snickered, "Nope."

Mole pulled out a chair and cringed as he put his foot on the chair to elevate it. "Let me ask you something."

"What?" Alex said, looking at him as if she did not want to have this conversation.

Mole knew that look and he didn't have the energy to fight with Alex this morning, "Do you like egg-white omelets?"

"Not really," she answered, forcing it down.

"Then why are you eating them?"

"Let me ask you something: do you do stuff for Anne that you don't like?" Alex asked. "There is no difference between what you do for Anne and what I do for Gastrix."

"For God's sake, Alex, do you even know his name?" Alex slammed her water on the table and could feel her arms start to tingle. She calmed down before she accidentally ignited in front of Mole.

"Forget it," Mole said. He turned his head to see Anne coming in. They kissed each other good morning and smiled.

Anne sat on the other side of the table across from where Mole had his foot elevated. "Morning, Alex."

Alex just nodded.

Anne turned to Kale. "Is everything okay?"

Mole opened his laptop to see a broken screen. "My laptop is busted, damn it. Anne, can I use yours?" Kale asked, showing her the screen.

"Mole just realized he was overstepping his boundary," Alex told Anne as she choked down another bite of omelet.

Mole slammed his laptop closed before he could get it started. "What the hell, Alex?! We have boundaries now? When did this happen?"

Alex stood up and put her plate in the dishwasher. "Damn it, Mole! Just come out and say what's on your mind."

"What the hell is going on with you? This guy is all wrong for you. He's an ass!" Mole said, pointing towards the bedroom. "He treats you like crap, and I would never have thought I would live to see the day that Alexandria Johnson would put up with all that from anyone."

"Not everyone can have a perfect little relationship like you have. Relationships take work," Alex started to get annoyed.

"He almost hit you last night, Alex," Mole yelled.

Alex rolled her eyes knowing full well Gastrix couldn't hurt her, "Oh, like you were all perfect when you were drinking. Do you not remember that car and a certain tree." Alex angrily got up from the table to put her bowl in the dishwasher. After she closed the door, she just turned around to stare at Mole.

Mole was just about to lose it when Anne stepped in, "Okay, okay, let's settle down. Let's relax."

Mole just stared at Alex and Alex glared back at him. Gastrix came into the kitchen. "Hey babe." He kissed her and patted her butt. "I'm sorry about last night. It's just that you know I love you so much and I don't want to lose you."

"It's okay, honey," she hugged him while looking at Mole who was giving her a look of anger.

"Kale," Anne said, putting her hand on his hand. "Kale."

Mole shook his head. "I don't have time for this." He opened his laptop, forgetting about his cracked screen. "Son of a bitch."

"Dude, your screen is cracked. Should take care of your stuff," Gastrix told him.

Anne grabbed his hand and squeezed as if telling Kale not to respond.

"Here is a computer company that Gastrix knows," Alex said, going into her purse and handing Mole the card. Mole took the card and handed it over to Anne, not taking his eyes off of Alex and Gastrix.

"I'll take care of it, honey," Anne said. "Come on, let me take you out to breakfast before your PT session."

126

Alex motioned sarcastically and waved off Mole. Mole literally bit his lip. "You know, Anne, I think I'm in the mood for a bowl of Fruity Pebbles and an Apollo. Suddenly, that sounds really, really, good." He painfully took his leg off the chair and walked out of the kitchen without his cane.

Anne grabbed his laptop and cane which was leaning against the wall by the door. She turned to look at Alex and Gastrix. "Dinner reservations are for this Saturday at six. I figure we will be there for drinks at 5:30."

"Good, looks like that man needs a few drinks in him," Gastrix said, grabbing Alex around the neck.

"Gastrix, Kale cannot drink alcohol, at all," Anne told him. "It's a mandatory jacket and tie." Anne started out of the kitchen before she turned around to Alex. "Please be on time." Anne's phone rang and she looked down at it. "It's my school. Excuse me, but I have to take this."

***

Sanah was on the rooftop of a building looking over the park. For a long time, his mind had been blurred, but tonight it had been cleared. He now knew what he was doing. Humanity doesn't deserve this world. He found himself loathing the people that he once protected.

Salamor joined him, "I need you to choose for them."

Sanah looked over the park at all the young college students pushing their agendas. "That one."

He pointed to one of the tables. "But first, I need to talk to someone."

"As you wish," Salamor whispered in his ear.

Sanah broke into the apartment where the little girl lived. He searched around the grimy living area but couldn't find any of the needles that killed her. He walked into her bedroom where he found multiple boxes of condoms. He opened the one that had been opened before. Inside was a couple of needles with a name, Cuegle.

***

Anne dropped Kale off at his physical therapy appointment. She checked him in at the front desk and helped him to the room. She headed off to drop Kale's computer off at the repair shop to get it fixed. Normally, she wouldn't take it to somewhere that Gastrix knew, but it was close to the Physical Therapy office.

"Chix Cyber Fix," Anne walked into the computer store where he saw two young girls behind the counter.

"Shelly," one girl said. "It's the cute innocent one."

Anne raised her eyebrows, "Excuse me, have we met?"

The other looked up, "Ah, still cute. And the flower is a nice touch."

Anne blushed, "I'm sorry, you look familiar, but I can't remember where I know you from."

"We are the girls who warned you about your friend dating Gastrix," Shelly said.

Anne realized who they were, "I apologize. I didn't recognize you."

"Quite all right. I'm Shelly. This is Tory."

Anne put her hand on her chest, "I'm Anne."

"Tory, her name is even cute," Shelly said.

A teenage boy came up from behind the doors to the back room. "Excuse me, but I'm having trouble bypassing the command structure."

Tory placed her hand on Shelly's arm, "I'll take care of this." The two of them imitated kisses towards each other.

"She's not only eye candy," Shelly said. She turned her attention back to Anne. "What brings you in?"

Anne put the laptop on the counter. Shelly opened it up and saw the screen crack. "Oh, poor baby," she grazed her finger across the screen. "What happened to her?"

"It fell off the dresser," Anne told her.

"Oh, honey."

Anne knew Shelly was talking to the computer. "Can you fix it?"

Shelly looked it over. "No, I don't think so. It would cost more than it's worth even if I could."

Anne sighed, "I guess I could order him one for his birthday."

"When is it?"

"What?"

"His birthday," Shelly asked.

"Saturday," Anne said. "Can you get the information from it?"

"That we can do," Shelly looked over at Anne. "What did you think of Gastrix?" she asked as she looked over the laptop.

Anne didn't know how to answer it, "I guess he makes my friend happy, so I guess I'm okay with it."

"So, they are still dating?" Shelly asked as she picked off a piece of the screen.

"Yep, and it is…challenging," she replied.

"He's a jackass."

"The laptop is a result of it," Anne admitted.

"Ah, I thought I recognized the work," Shelly playfully grinned.

"What do you know of him?" Anne asked.

"Tory, can you come out here for a second?" Shelly yelled to the back room.

Tory came out drinking a soda, "We really need to teach him how to bypass the command structure. What's up?"

"Anne would like to know about Gastrix," Shelly said.

"Oh, you mean Rumpelstiltskin," Tory said. "He's an ass."

"Why do you call him Rumpelstiltskin?" Anne asked.

"His real name is Eugene Lewis," Tory said. "For some reason he hates it. I found out because, well I went through his wallet." Tory then added, "He was dating my sister and I wanted to…put a…. let's just say…the police department's computer system may have input that he was wanted for sexual misconduct with some sheep in Montana."

Anne laughed, "What?"

"So, one night, he was drinking, and I had no proof he was beating my sister, so I wanted to see if he had been."

"What did you do?"

"I called him Eugene," Tory admitted.

"What happened?"

Tory turned around and lifted her hair to see a bunch of scars on the back of her neck. "He grabbed my throat and threw me into a light on the wall. I got burns and scars from the glass."

"I'm sorry," Anne said, looking down.

"Not your fault, dear," Shelly said.

"No charges were pressed?" Anne asked.

"My sister lied to the cops about what happened, so it was two stories to mine alone…and I don't have the greatest police record."

"Tory," the boy's voice cried from the back room.

She rolled her eyes, "I swear if this kid had half a brain, he'd be dangerous." She turned to go to the backroom. "What?!" she playfully screamed.

"She is so hot," Shelly said, looking at her as she walked away. "Anyways, about your little predicament." She picked up the laptop. "I can build you a custom-made laptop"

"How much will that cost?" Anne asked.

"How about the dealer's cost of the parts?" Shelly said. "Labor and markup will be on the house?"

"Really? Why?" Anne asked.

"One, you have enough troubles with the jackass and two, just promise me that you'll get him out of your friend's life," she asked. "In all seriousness…he's not a good man."

***

Sanah walked out to the table in the park that he chose for the purpose. There were many vendors in the park, but he knew these folks already had some influence of the Dark in them even though they didn't know it. He walked up to the man holding an F.O.R. pamphlet. "Dude, are you interested in getting religion out of our government and influencing our kids to murdering propaganda?"

"I promise, I will talk to you later but right now I need some information," Sanah told him. "Where can I find the man who distributes these?" He held up the needles and the name of the man who distributed the narcotics that killed the little girl.

***

"Why do I have to buy a suit and jacket for someone else's party?" Gastrix asked. "This conforms into how white America wants you to dress and wants you to think."

"Think about it, we dress certain ways for the club, think of this as a club and we follow the dress schemes," Alex pointed out. She moved her new brightly neon red hair out of the way. "Besides, I would like you to go." She held up a jacket and tie. "I like this combination."

"Whatever, but we are not going to stay long," Gastrix said. "We need to put this on your charge account until I get paid on the first of the month."

"Yah, that's fine," Alex was a little worried about what the church was going to say regarding that month's bill. "We need to find a shirt and pants as well."

"And shoes, socks, and belt," Gastrix added.

132

"Okay," Alex said. She caught herself in the mirror. She stared at herself as she ran her fingers through her new hair color and style. "I guess I can grow to love it."

After Alex paid for the outfit for him to wear at Mole's birthday dinner, they walked through town. It was busy as people were shopping and laughing. Komptin kept on trying to get in between Gastrix and Alex but Alex had enough of it. She pushed him so he had to stay behind her on his leash. Alex looked ahead and saw a welcome set of faces.

"Celestial," Alex said, giving a quick minor bow.

"Alexandria," Celestial said, giving her a big hug. "How are you doing?"

"I'm fine." Alex peered over to see Ariel and Devine, both of them eating ice cream. Alex found herself a little envious of the two angels. "Ariel, Devine,"

The two of them just nodded as they ate their ice cream cones.

"Who," Ariel was studying him.

"Or what?" Devine said as she pointed up and down at Gastrix.

"Is this?" they both concluded.

"Oh, I'm sorry, this is Gastrix," Alex told them.

Ariel and Devine choked on their ice cream which Alex thought was odd because they didn't breathe.

Celestial reached behind her to grab the ice cream toppings out of her hair. She turned to them, "Be open." Celestial turned to Gastrix. "I am Celestial." She extended her arm. Gastrix shook her hand and she placed her other hand on top of his hand. "It is nice to meet you."

"Gastrix, music extraordinaire, listen to beats I dare. I don't conform to your way, don't listen to me and you'll pay," he bragged to himself.

Ariel and Devine struggled to keep themselves from laughing out loud.

"Excuse me," Celestial said out of confusion.

"I lay down beats for my peeps," he started spouting off.

"Oh my God," Ariel commented.

"This just gets better," Devine finished. The two of them continued to eat their ice cream as if watching a show.

Alex shot them a dirty look. Komptin walked up to Celestial as she knelt down and generated a dog treat from her hand. She fed it to him, "I miss him as well." She placed her head on Komptin's head.

Alex got a look of worry on her face. "Is he not happy with me?"

Gastrix looked at Alex, "It's a dog, he's happy as long as he eats."

Celestial got up and grabbed Alex's hand. "Come with me, please."

Alex started to walk with Celestial when Gastrix started to follow her. Ariel and Devine quickly stepped in and put their hands on Gastrix.

"What?" Gastrix said. He turned around, annoyed. "Doesn't matter. She will tell me anyways."

"Doubt it," the two of them said simultaneously.

Celestial interlocked her arm with Alex. "How are you doing?"

"I'm fine," Alex looked back at Gastrix to see where he was. "I didn't think I would meet the one you were so reluctant to tell me about so quickly."

"Are you happy?" Celestial asked, studying her.

Alex didn't answer right away, "Yes."

Celestial gave a loving mother's smile, "Be careful when opening doors, you might be surprised what is on the other side."

Alex didn't really pay attention to what Celestial was saying as she was worried about Gastrix. She was afraid to say anything that would upset him. "What about Komptin?" Alex looked back at her dog out of worry. "Is he not happy with me?" Alex almost didn't get the next words out. "If he is with me because of a promise to Osiah; I don't want him too miserable."

"Alexandria, he loves you and will die for you in a moment's notice," Celestial said. "Do not ever worry about that." She looked over at Ariel and Devine. "But he is worried about you."

"I get it," Alex said. "I had a fight with my brother this morning. Gastrix and I just got done with a big fight because we ran into Sanah. He thought Sanah and I were sleeping together."

Celestial stopped in her tracks. "Sanah. Sanah is here."

"Yes, we ran into each other a little bit ago. He is a really good hunter," Alex pointed out.

"Best I have ever seen," Celestial commented. "He had such a beautiful family."

Alex couldn't believe what she heard, "What do you mean had?

"A demon tortured and murdered his wife and son," Celestial said. "He buried himself in the hunt to make sure their deaths would not be in vain."

"I didn't know, he told me he writes them," Alex said. Then she realized that it was probably just his way to deal with the loss. "I didn't know."

"And that is how I live to work on my music," Gastrix told Ariel and Devine as they stood there dumbfounded, letting their ice cream melt over their hands.

Ariel and Devine both turned their heads to greet Celestial. They both shook their heads as they said, "Wow."

Celestial turned to Alex, "I have to go, my dear, but we will see you again." She kissed her on her forehead. Alex watched her disappear into the crowd.

"Who was she?" Gastrix asked.

"She's kind of like my work mom," Alex said. "She looks out for me."

"What did she say to you?" Gastrix asked.

"Just asked about work," Alex said.

"I don't like you lying to me," he reminded her.

She turned to him and kissed him. "I know, baby."

***

Sanah approached a crappy looking house in the rough part of town. He heard a man yelling at some kids to be quiet. Sanah knocked on the door and a young woman in her mid-twenties opened it.

"Yes?" she asked, looking at him. She looked around to make sure there were no cops in the area.

"I'm looking for the guy who deals with these," he held up the needles.

"Are you a cop?" the lady asked.

"Nope, looking for a hit," Sanah told her.

She opened the door. "Come on in."

Sanah walked into the house where there were kids who were malnourished and wearing dirty diapers. The house was dirty, and the smell of a mixture of rotten food and urine filled the rooms. He walked into the kitchen where a man was playing cards with three other guys.

"What do you want?"

Sanah held up the needles, "I want more of these."

"It's a hundred a hit, let's see the cash," he said, placing a gun on the table. The three other guys placed guns on the table.

Sanah looked around as the mom was yelling at the kids to be quiet. "Let's see the needles."

"Cash first."

Sanah pulled the cash out of his jacket pocket and placed it on the table. "There should be 800, count it."

One of the guys picked it up and counted as Sanah kept staring at the boss. "Yo, Hans, there is $840.00."

"Consider it a tip if the product is good," Sanah told him.

"Best there is, man." The man got up and picked up some kid's cereal. He pulled out eight needles and handed it over to him. "Your money is good here anytime."

Sanah looked at the needles. "Do you mind if I shoot up really quick?"

"Mi casa su casa," the man said, picking up his cards. "I raise 25." He threw his chips onto the table.

Sanah took off his jacket and rolled up his sleeve.

"Hey man, where's your tracks?" one of the guys asked.

"Watch this," Sanah said. He lit up his fist and punched the first guy in the face, smashing through to the back of the skull. The sound of kids screaming filled the house as Sanah used his power to push the boss away from his weapon. He flew through the wall, screaming. The two others got up and Sanah formed a knife, jabbing it into the eye socket of one of them. The last guy standing begged for forgiveness. Sanah grabbed the crucifix from his neck and ripped it off.

"I'm sorry, please, I'm sorry," the man pleaded.

"I'm not," Sanah formed a spear and thrust it into his heart and the man dropped on the table, covered in drugs and money. Sanah walked into the room where the boss had landed.

"Go to Hell, you piece of shit," the man spat at Sanah.

"See you there," Sanah said as he formed a spear and jabbed it through the head of his victim. The man's body laid on the floor twitching as Sanah got off of him. Sanah walked back through the kitchen and into the living room where the kids were hiding alone. Their mother was nowhere in sight. "Find the mother, kill her." Sanah spoke to the infiltrators as he walked out of the house, "The

138

children...just do it fast and painless." The infiltrators walked into the living room as the kids screamed and then suddenly silenced.

***

Anne helped Kale out of the car as he tried to lift himself out. "You all right?"

"I'm good," Kale said, trying to hide the pain in his back. "You look beautiful."

Anne smiled, "Thank you, but I'm nervous."

"Why?"

"Because everyone is going to be looking at me and ask why I am with the most handsome, generous, funny, and best man in the room," Anne told him.

Kale laughed at Anne, "We've come a long way since that night on the lake beach."

Anne remembered that night, "It all started with you giving me your sweatshirt. I knew right then and there that there was more to Kale Moler than he lets on, and I'm the lucky woman who you let see it."

Kale kissed her, "I don't know where I would be without you."

"Stop being so mushy," Dan said behind him. A girl came out the passenger side of Dan's vehicle. "Oh, I'm sorry. This is Jessica."

Anne and Kale greeted Jessica. "You were at Distance the night we were there?" Anne asked her.

"Yes," Jessica said. "I woke up next to Dan that next morning and thought, what the hell, let's see why I went home with him." Jessica grabbed Dan's hand. "I'm glad I did."

139

"That's sweet," Anne said. "Come on, let's go inside and check in."

"Happy birthday, buddy," Dan said as they walked into the restaurant.

"Thanks, man," Mole said to him.

"Yeah, sure thing," Dan adjusted his tie as he watched Jessica and Anne walk ahead of them. "How have you been feeling?"

"Sore, but manageable, thanks to my live-in nurse I have," Mole said. "Still not getting the sponge bath, though."

"I'm sure Dan would help you with that," Anne yelled ahead of them.

The four of them reached the top floor of the restaurant and to Mole's surprise, his mom was there with her new boyfriend. She ran over and gave her son a hug. "Oh, honey, how are you feeling?"

"Good, mom," Mole said. "So glad you're here. Nice to see you again, Victor."

Victor put out his hand, "Kale, you look good."

"Thanks," he said. "Where's Alex?"

"Haven't seen her," his mom said.

"Think she'll come?" Kale asked Anne.

"Why wouldn't she?" his mom asked him.

"We kind of had a fight this morning, a big one," Mole admitted to his mom.

Anne rubbed Kale's back, "She'll be here, honey."

"What did you fight about?" Dan asked. "You guys were two peas in a pod and never fought."

Anne got a text, she looked at it, "She said she's running late but will be here by six."

"Mom, you will see what we were fighting about at six," Mole said. "Come on, let's go see the rest of the guests."

Mole and Anne were talking at the bar. Mole decided to treat himself to a Coke. They sat around laughing and Mole was telling the story about him falling off the treadmill making fun of himself. The elevator opened and Kameron came up to him.

"Sorry I'm late," Kameron said. "But my appointment lasted longer than I expected."

"No problem," Mole said. "Mom, Victor, this is Kameron."

"Oh," Kate said. She gave him a big hug and kissed him on the cheek. "That is for helping my son at the hospital."

"Ma'am, it was no trouble at all," Kameron told her.

"Can I get you a drink?" Mole asked.

"I'd love to, but I just had enough time to stop in to wish you a happy birthday and to let you know that I have to move out tonight."

"What? Why?" Mole asked.

"My credits came through and it turned out I had enough to graduate already," he said. "And I just got notified I have to leave for a training course tomorrow." Kameron looked at his watch. "In fact, I have to get going and pack."

"Oh man, well, congratulations on early graduation," Mole said. "Let me walk you out." Mole got up, limping over and Anne handed his cane over to him. "Thank you," Kale said.

***

141

Anne watched Kale walk Kameron to the elevator.

"You love him, don't you?" Kate asked with a loving mother's smile.

Anne turned her head over to his mom, "Like no other."

"There's something wrong though, isn't there?" Kale's mom noticed.

"Yes but no. I wish I could tell you, but I need to talk to Kale first," she said.

"Are you pregnant?"

"No," Anne was calculating in her head. "Not that I know of."

"Well, I'm sure whatever it is, I'm sure you two can manage to get through it," she said. "He'd never admit it, but he's loved you ever since you two graduated high school."

"I'm a lucky girl," Anne admitted. Anne watched Kameron leave down the stairs of the restaurant after Kale gave Kameron a quick hug. The elevator opened to Alex with Gastrix. "That's the reason for Kale and Alex's fight."

***

The first thing Kale noticed was Alex had changed her long, weaved hair to a new neon red hair style. She looked awful. "Happy birthday," Alex said to him. She gave him a quick hug, but Mole felt it distant and just going through the motions. After a quick release she handed him a card.

Mole took the card from Alex, "Thank you." He smiled at her, but she did a half return as she walked to the bar to talk with Mole's mom and her boyfriend. Mole watched her laugh and smile as she made the rounds with Gastrix at her side. She was showing off her hair to the people around it. Mole was joined by Anne.

"Still fighting?" she asked.

Mole held up the card. It was a generic card that said, "Happy Birthday from Alexandria and Gastrix." Inside the card was a twenty-dollar gift certificate to Wal-Mart. "I guess so," Anne said. She put one hand up on Mole's shoulders, "Come on. Try to have a good time, this fight won't last long."

"I guess you're right," Mole said. He turned around. "We've never fought before, not like this." He looked over at Gastrix who was getting a drink from the bar, probably with Alex's credit card. "I don't like him."

Anne gave her man a quick hug from the back, "Go on. Go try to have fun."

***

Mole was actually having a good time talking to Dan and his mom's boyfriend. Just prior to the conversation, Dan and Mole were video chatting with Robbie over in Minnesota. It was nice of him to call Mole on the night of his party. It made Mole feel pretty good that he was doing well since Sara's death.

Dan got Mole another Coke as Dan was looking over at Gastrix, "What the hell does she see him?" He got another drink and handed it to Jessica.

143

"Thank you," Jessica said. She returned to talk to Kale's mom and her boyfriend.

"No clue, dude," Mole replied. "He's a putz."

Dan put his drink on the bar, "Man, the seal is about to break." He started to look around. He turned to the bartender, "Hey, where's the restroom?

"Down the hall, plunger is under the sink," the bald bartender said.

"Thanks, man," Dan walked up the hall to the bathroom.

Mole looked over at the bartender in confusion who was continuing to serve drinks. Mole continued to look over the crowd as he was waiting for dinner to start. He was getting kind of hungry. He tried everything he could to prevent himself from rolling his eyes as Gastrix came up to him.

"Hey, man," Gastrix ordered another round of drinks.

"How's it going?" Mole said, looking around for Anne or Dan to save him from having to talk to Gastrix.

"Oh, you know, little woman wants a refill and so she made me come get it," Gastrix told him. "Oh, the things I do for her."

"It's just amazing," Mole looked over at Alex. The two made eye contact and she quickly turned away with a cold look in her eyes.

"You look tense, man, you need to relax," Gastrix said. "You need a drink." He motioned to the bartender.

"I can't drink," Mole said, still looking for a way out.

Mole's phone rang and he saw that Anne's parents were calling. "Excuse me, but I need to take this."

"Do what you gotta do," Gastrix said. He watched him walk away, talking on the phone as he went up to his girlfriend, pointing to the phone. Gastrix looked at Mole's drink that he had left sitting on the bar. He asked for a shot of vodka as he poured it into Mole's drink. "Dude needs to chill," he thought to himself.

***

Anne returned to talking to her parents and she gave Mole back his phone. He continued to look at his glass of pop. "What's wrong?"

"Coke is flat," Mole said. "It tastes weird." He continued to drink it.

"Do you want a new one?" Anne asked.

Mole chugged the rest of it down, "Nope, but for some reason I like the taste of it." He looked over to the bar. "I think I'll have another."

Gastrix came up to him, "I'll get it for you."

Alex came up to Anne and Mole, "That's nice of you, honey." She gave Mole a look as if showing off she was right and then turned back to talking with Dan.

Mole snarled back at her. He felt Anne squeeze his hand, "Stop it," she told him.

"What?" Mole said. Gastrix came back with the drinks and Mole tasted it. "Good, they haven't changed the carbonation yet.," he said, drinking it.

The hostess came in to inform everyone that their table was ready. Anne grabbed Mole's arm and guided him to the table. She felt his hands grab her butt cheek, "Come on, baby," he said to her.

"Kale," she said, knocking his hand off. "Stop it."

Throughout dinner, people were engaged in relative conversation, except Mole and Alex. They were not even looking at each other. Anne could tell Mole was getting more and more upset as the night was going on because he kept on getting louder, and Anne would hate to say it, a bit more obnoxious. Anne was trying to keep him under control, but he was too upset with Alex to have a good night. She could tell that Alex told Gastrix to try to make friends as he was getting drinks for everyone all night.

Dinner was over and Mole's mom was giving Anne dirty looks all through the dessert. She knew Mole's mom was not happy with her for something. Her stomach was in knots knowing that she did something to upset his mom.

"Speech," Dan said, tapping on the side of his glass.

Mole stood up and tapped the glass so hard it broke. He laughed as he said, "Oh damn," loud enough for the tables around them to hear him.

Anne was starting to feel a little embarrassed as she tried to quiet him down, "Kale."

"Don't worry, honey buns," he said. "You can give me the good-loving tonight."

Anne's face turned beet red as she could tell that everyone was shocked at Mole's behavior. Anne noticed the only one laughing was Gastrix.

"I just wanted to say that, well, this past couple of months have been just truly horrible. If it hadn't been for my pretty little flower here, I don't know what I do," he leaned over and obnoxiously kissed her in front of everyone. She managed to somewhat push him off of her.

"Dan, you are a great friend. Mom couldn't have asked for anyone better to raise me. Alex, you're my best friend and a great sister, when you are not being such a close-minded bitch."

Alex's face turned beet red too and Anne almost thought she could see a hint of blue coming from underneath the table as she gave Mole a look of death. The table was quiet as Mole sat down, spilling water on Anne. She quickly grabbed the napkin and wiped it off.

"I gotta drain my vein," Mole said. "I may need some help holding it," he motioned to Anne.

"Just go," Anne said, completely annoyed.

Anne got up and went to the bar, asking for more napkins to wipe her dress off when she felt a strong woman's grip on her arm, turning her around.

"What the hell do you think you are doing?" Mole's mom asked.

Anne shockingly replied, "I don't know what you are talking about."

"He's plastered!" Mole's mom said. "When did he start drinking again?" His mom was at a loss for words as she bit her bottom lip. "Damn it, Anne, I thought you were smarter than this and more responsible."

"What? I don't know what you're talking about," Anne said. "He hasn't had a drink since we've been together, I swear."

147

The bartender came to Anne and handed her a napkin and the bar bill, "I have to cut your husband off."

"He's not my husband, he's my... wait, what?" Anne stopped wiping the water off herself. She looked at the bill, "357 dollars!!" Anne said. "All he ordered was Coke?! And it was flat at that."

"He's been drinking coke with vodka all night, if he doesn't settle up the bill and leave, we are going to have to call the police," he told them.

Anne quickly turned to Mole's mom, "I swear, I didn't know."

Mole's mom pulled out her wallet. "I believe you." She paid the bill. "But now we have a problem on our hands."

Anne turned to the bartender, "Did my husband order those drinks?"

"No, his friend did. The one with the messed-up hair," the bartender pointed to Gastrix.

Chapter 8

Anne, along with Kate's boyfriend, went to the bathroom to get Mole. Mole came out with vomit all over his suit. "Anne, I feel funny," he said, falling on the floor, managing to get back into the bathroom to vomit again.

The manager of the restaurant came up to them. "You need to get him out of here before I call the police. We are not this type of establishment and you will not be returning. Now pay your bill and leave," the manager said, handing over the table bills.

"Don't worry about this, Anne, I will take care of the bills. Just take care of Kale," his mom's boyfriend said.

Alex and Gastrix came up to Anne, "Is he all right?"

Anne did everything possible not to yell, but she snapped "He's fine."

Alex walked by, "Too bad, he's lucky I didn't knock the daylight out of him," Alex commented. "We're heading out." Gastrix waved by to Anne as he wrapped his arms around Alex's neck.

Mole's mom walked up to Anne, "How long has Alex been like that?"

"Since him," Anne said. She looked to the bathroom as she heard Kale vomiting. She grabbed her phone.

"Who are you calling?" Mole's mom asked.

"Kale's doctor," Anne said. "I need to make sure if Kale will be alright mixing his pills with alcohol." More sounds of vomit came from the bathroom. Anne just shook her head, worried about what this was going to lead to.

***

It took Anne, Kate, and Victor to carry Kale up the stairs and lay him in the bathroom.

"I'm going to have to stay up with him," Anne said. She knelt down and rubbed his vomit-soaked hair. She got up and washed her hands.

The sound of Alex getting home with Gastrix caught Anne's attention. "Smells like someone ralphed," Gastrix said out loud. Anne was about to lose her cool when she walked into the living room. Gastrix and Alex were on the couch, turning on the TV.

Anne turned to Mole's mom. "Do you mind going to the supermarket and getting some 7-Up for Kale…and take your time," Anne asked them.

"Of course, honey," she answered. "If you need anything, just call." She motioned for her boyfriend to follow.

Anne waited until they left the house and shut the door. Anne grabbed the remote from Gastrix's hand to shut the TV off and threw it on the chair. "We are going to talk," Anne said.

"Hey there's a good anime on I wanted to watch," Gastrix told her.

"That's nice, but it's not happening now and it's not happening here," Anne said. "I'm only going to ask this question once, and you better listen because I want a straight answer."

Gastrix rolled his eyes, "What?"

"Do you remember me telling you that Kale cannot have any alcohol?"

"I guess," Gastrix said.

Anne was getting tenser because she was afraid of the answer to her next question. "Did you, I repeat, did you give him coke with vodka all night tonight?"

"Anne, this is stupid," Alex said, trying to get up.

Anne quickly motioned for her to sit down, "Alex, this does not concern you right now." She never turned her attention away from Gastrix. "I want an answer."

"He needed to relax, so I gave him some drinks to make sure he had a good time. I didn't know he was going to act like an ass and insult Alex. Which made her feel like crap, by the way. I hope he can apologize to her," Gastrix said, going to his phone.

"You don't see anything that you did was wrong?" Anne asked. She turned to Alex, "Do you?"

"Anne, it was a mistake, he didn't know he was a recovering alcoholic," Alex said.

Anne rolled her eyes, "Regardless of the fact that I said he can't drink alcohol, or you didn't know he was a recovering alcoholic, are you telling me he didn't know what would happen if he poured alcohol into a person's drink who is on pain medication without him knowing?" She turned to Gastrix, "Are you that naïve?"

Gastrix stood up to look Anne in her face, "Look, I don't know what you just called me, and I'm going to take it to the fact that you are more upset at your boyfriend making an ass out of himself and insulting my girl, his sister. So, we are going to bed and maybe with some sleep you will apologize to us in the morning," Gastrix told her, pulling Alex up off the couch.

The sound of Kale vomiting in the toilet came from down the hall, "Anne," Kale moaned.

"Get out," Anne said to Gastrix. "Get out of my house. You are not welcome here."

"You can't kick him out," Alex now stepped up to Anne. "Why are you being so mean to him? It was an honest mistake!"

"Alex, are you actually defending his actions?" Anne shouted back.

"Not everyone can be perfect like you," Alex said. "People make mistakes."

"Are you serious?!" Anne questioned back. "Alex, can't you see he is dragging you down with him?"

"You don't talk to her like that about me," Gastrix pointed to Anne, gritting his teeth. "I take no disrespect from no girl."

"Get out of my house," Anne pointed to the door. "Now."

"You don't tell me what to do," Gastrix said.

Anne walked over to the door and opened it, "Get out now."

"Suck it, bitch," Gastrix yelled at her. He sat back down on the chair. Alex sat on Gastrix's lap, picking up the remote.

Anne had finally lost it. She went over to the TV and unplugged it. "Out." Gastrix picked Alex up and threw her on the couch. He took the remote and threw it against the TV, breaking both the TV and remote. He grabbed Anne by the throat and was about to swing when Komptin came into the room. He growled and barked at Gastrix before he could swing at Anne.

Gastrix looked over at the dog who looked as if he was going to pounce at him. He let Anne go. "Don't ever treat me like that again."

"You are never welcome here," Anne said. "Now get out." She pointed to the door.

"If he goes, I go," Alex said.

"Alex, please, look at this situation you are in. Look at him," she pleaded. "Look at what he's doing to you."

"Go to Hell, Anne," Alex was in complete anger. She got up from the couch and grabbed Gastrix's hand. He batted it away and walked out the door. "You shouldn't have made him mad. This is all your and Mole's fault."

Anne just shook her head. "Alex, when you need us, we'll be here."

"I will never need you," Alex said. "Gastrix is my boyfriend, he's all I need," she stormed up, walking out the door. "Komptin, come." Komptin reluctantly came to Alex's side. He looked at Anne and put his head down as he walked out the door.

"Anne," Kale cried from the bathroom. "I think there was something wrong with my dinner." The sound of Kale vomiting was a clue into what she was in for the night.

***

Sanah was surrounded by infiltrators. The fact that he had killed so many didn't affect him one bit. He was actually feeling rather comfortable being in

153

their surroundings. They were dark, they smelled, but they had a sense of loyalty to him. They respected what he was capable of doing.

Salamor approached Sanah who was overlooking the city from the warehouse. "There hasn't been any sign of the Sentry for quite some time," he hissed.

Sanah replied, "Her priorities are to herself. She is as much a threat as a mosquito is to an elephant. She's useless." Sanah turned his attention to Salamor. "I'm going to go get you the first."

"As you wish," Salamor said. "I have something I must go check on."

***

"I really don't feel good," Mole commented to Anne who was sitting next to him at the kitchen table.

"You had a rough night," Anne said, getting him some Gatorade.

"What happened?" Mole asked, grabbing his head. "Could you get me something for my head?"

Anne got up and got him some pills and water. "You know that medication you're on?"

"Yeah," Mole said, trying not to talk too loudly.

"Well, I guess I need to just say it, you mixed them with alcohol," Anne said, handing him the pills. "Vodka to be exact."

"I drank last night?" Mole said. "Great. Over 3 years sobriety down the drain," he felt as if he was a failure. "Anne, I don't remember even wanting, ordering, or anyone allowing me to drink."

Anne looked as disappointed in herself as Mole was in himself, "Honey, you didn't know you were drinking. I didn't know you were either."

"Then how?" Mole asked.

"Gastrix was giving it to you in your Coke without you knowing," Anne said.

"Oh, he's a piece of work," Mole said. "Well, if any good comes out of this, it will be that Alex will have a good reason to dump his ass." He looked around, "Where is she anyways? She normally doesn't take this long taking Komptin for a walk."

Anne sighed as she said, "She left last night with Gastrix. I don't think she is coming back."

"What did I say last night?" he asked.

"Well, at dinner, you kind of called her a bitch in front of everyone at the table," Anne said. "But that's not the reason she is gone."

"What happened?"

Anne took a sip of her coffee, "I asked Gastrix to leave and not come back." Mole could see Anne was upset over something as she rubbed her neck. "And Alex went with him."

Mole picked up his phone.

"Who are you calling?" Anne asked.

"Alex," Mole said. "We are going to get this cleared up quickly before it is too late." Mole listened to the message on the other end of the phone, and he felt all the blood leave his face as he felt he was going to vomit.

"What's wrong," Anne asked.

"She discontinued her number," Mole said. "I'm pretty sure she is done with us." Mole looked up at Anne. "I didn't do anything last night to upset you, did I?"

Anne shook her head no, "Of course not."

***

Alex was looking at her new phone she purchased. "I like this phone." She looked at Komptin who was walking by her side. She sat down on the bench in the park as she was playing with her new phone. She looked over at Komptin who was lying down by her feet but was a little farther away than usual. "I know you are upset. We've haven't had a hunt for quite some time," she pointed out. "Tell you what, I'll go with Gastrix to the club for a little while and I'll come home, and we can go out and see what kind of trouble we can get into."

She scooted over to Komptin and gave him a quick little pet on the head. She texted Gastrix her new phone number. "You know, I should have put him on my account as well." Komptin looked up at her. "He's shows me such love." She got up from the bench. "Come on, Komptin. Let's go get him some breakfast."

***

Sanah watched the Sentry get up from the bench. He knew that he couldn't let her know his intentions because even though she didn't care about the mission, it would be a reason just to fight. He saw the first individual over by the table pushing the pamphlets to people as they were walking by.

He walked up to the guy holding a pamphlet with an upside number four on it. The man asked, "I remember you; did you want to join Freedom Off Religion?"

"I'm interested in not just joining but to help you in such ways that you can't possibly fathom," Sanah said. He handed him a piece of paper with an address on it. "Meet me here tonight and I will help you and the cause."

"Sounds good, man," the man gave thumbs up to him.

***

Anne had to get some stuff done for school while Mole went out for a walk. He needed to get some fresh air. It was getting late and the sun was going down. He decided he wanted to go out and get a greasy burger. For some reason having a greasy burger with french fries had always helped his stomach getting over a hangover.

He came up to a convenience store where he picked up a Coke to drink on his walk. The pain in his back was hurting him all day from lying on the bathroom floor. He couldn't remember the last time his body wasn't in pain. Then he remembered when he didn't feel any pain and that was last night. He knew that last night shouldn't have happened, but he hadn't felt that good for a long time.

The next thing Mole knew he was holding a small bottle of vodka in his hand. A voice came to his head, "One little bottle won't hurt, you conquered it last night."

Mole caught himself talking out loud, "I really shouldn't; I have a disease."

"The only thing to make you feel no pain," the voice said.

"I can't," Mole said, putting it down, but then he picked it up again, reading the label on the vodka bottle. "No." He paid for his Coke and left the store.

***

It was late by the time that the F.O.R. representative finally got to Sanah's apartment. Sanah opened the door and in front of him was the man with a young lady.

"Hey, man, sorry I'm late but we were getting ready to go out tonight," the guy said. "I'm Jack and this is my girlfriend Cheri."

"Nice to meet you," Sanah said, shaking their hands. "Please, come in." Sanah watched the two attempt to take their shoes off. "No need to take your shoes off. Please, have a seat."

"So how can we help you?" Jack asked as he made himself comfortable.

"Would you like something to drink?" Sanah asked.

"Whatever you have would be great."

Cheri spoke, "Just water for me. Got to hydrate up for tonight." The two of them laughed, no doubt preparing for a wild night ahead of them.

Sanah had something they were not expecting. "So, tell me about your organization," Sanah asked, making himself some hot tea.

"Well, F.O.R. is an organization that wants to take religion completely out of this country. Religion is a manmade cult that has infiltrated our government, schools, and daily lives that corrupt its people to murder in their names. We should be free of religion so we can live our lives with true freedom."

"So, you're not interested in one religion, you want to get rid of all religions?" Sanah confirmed with them. "A truly noble cause."

"Thank you," Jack said. "We are growing stronger and stronger every day. We actually hit over 50 people in the local area and a new faction growing in the D.C. area."

"You said 50 in the local area?" Sanah inquired.

"Fifty strong and growing," Jack pointed out.

"I would like to help your cause," Sanah said, sipping his hot tea. "I can make your organization stronger than you can possibly hope."

"How can you do that?" Cheri asked.

"Only the truly dedicated can know that answer," Sanah said getting up. "If I were to offer you this power, how do I know that you are true?"

Jack was getting all excited, "We are true, no matter what."

"Okay," Sanah said. "I just need you to do one little thing for me. I'm going to open this door and behind it is something that is truly frightful but if you accept, you will have power with your organization like no other."

Cheri and Jack stood up and looked at each other, "We swear it." they both said.

"No matter what is behind this door?"

"No matter what," Cheri said.

Sanah nodded and opened the door. A room of three infiltrators were turned to the two kids. "Only need two," Sanah said.

"What are those?" the girl asked, studying them.

"True power," Jack answered him.

Sanah looked to the kids. "Do you accept?"

"Yes," Cheri said, opening her arms.

"Yes," Jack said, dropping to his knees.

"Now," Sanah told the infiltrators. They leaped at the two kids, opening themselves up to them. The screams of being infiltrated echoed throughout Sanah's head. He shook it off as the two rose from the experience.

"And who are we now?" Sanah asked them to clear out his ears.

"You call me Velcrown," Jack said.

"I am now Welltore," the girl replied.

"Welcome," Sanah said. "Go, I will call you when ready for phase two." Their eyes flashed red as they turned to the door. "We will grow our army to stop this war."

***

Alex stopped in her tracks as she sensed what had just happened. She hadn't had that smell of stale air since the night Sara's dad was infiltrated. She looked down at Komptin who in turn looked at her, flashing his blue eyes.

"What's wrong?" Gastrix asked. "We need to eat for a wild night tonight."

160

"I don't know if I should," Alex said, looking around. "I really should go to work tonight."

"The church, on a night like this?" Gastrix said. "No, you are coming with me to the club. After last night, I need to relax, and I can't relax if you're out goofing around on me."

"I really should go in," Alex said. Her attention was now to see what was behind her.

Gastrix got all tense. "Look, I'm looking at you from the outside and I know better than you can see. You are going out so we can relax."

"Okay, but not a late night, okay?" Alex asked.

Gastrix kissed her on top of her head, "We'll see."

Komptin growled and barked loudly. "Komptin," Alex said. "Stop it."

"It's going to be hard to find a place that will take that dog, we may have to get rid of it," Gastrix pointed.

"That is something I can't and will not do," Alex told him.

"It's a dog," Gastrix said.

"Gastrix, there is something I need to tell you about Komptin and myself," Alex said. "Something that I don't know that you will believe."

"What's that?" he said, lighting up a cigarette, leaning on a building.

"Gastrix, I'm a..." Alex tried to say when Komptin started to bark. "Komptin, hush," Alex told him. "Anyways, as I was saying, I'm a..." Alex tried to say until Komptin pushed Alex with his body, knocking her over. "Damn it, Komptin. "Alex regained her posture. "Now stop it," Alex fixed her clothes. "Gastrix, Komptin and I are..."

161

Alex stopped herself as she saw Mole walking down the street drinking a Coke.

Mole looked up and met eyes with Alex. The two just looked at each other when Gastrix looked over at Mole. Alex just turned to Gastrix. "Let's go." She grabbed his arm and dragged Gastrix off.

***

"You lost your best friend," the voice said to Mole.

"Yes, I did," he agreed with it.

"Does it hurt?"

"Worst pain I ever felt," Mole told it.

"You know how to mend the pain," the voice told him.

Mole went back to the liquor store and grabbed a bottle of whiskey. "I never really cared for vodka." He went to the clerk. "I will take this and a pack of gum." Mole put the gum in his pocket and opened the bottle.

The clerk stopped him, "You can't drink that here."

"Yeah, okay," Mole turned away and opened the bottle and started chugging it. "Oh God, this tastes good."

"It gets better with every sip," the voice told him.

Mole continued to drink as he walked out the door.

***

Anne didn't realize how long Kale was gone. She was busy writing her application for what the school asked her to do. She felt guilty not telling Kale about the opportunity for her to study in the Vatican for six months. She knew six months wouldn't be that long, but right now as it was laying out, Kale would be here alone. She knew Alex was headstrong and would not be coming back to them. Kale was equally as headstrong. He's been gone awhile, she thought. She picked up her phone and saw a message for him come through saying he went to a late movie.

"Sounds good, love you," she texted him. She didn't know if she should leave him for six months. Would they break up? Would they grow apart? The only thing Anne knew was she was in love with Kale Moler, but this was an opportunity of a lifetime. She continued to write her application. It wouldn't hurt to finish it to even see if they would accept her to the study.

**

Mole was feeling pretty good at the strip club. It wasn't that he was looking for one, it was just the nearest bar he came across. He hadn't felt this good for a long time. He took out another hundred dollars from the ATM. He asked some of the girls to exchange them for some singles.

"You wanna come in the back for a private party?" the girl asked.

"No, I'm just here to experience it all," Mole said. "But here is a dollar for just being gorgeous."

163

"Why, thank you," the girl said. "And here is a present for you for being the best looking, kindest man in the club tonight." She put her arms around him to give him a kiss on the cheek. "You're sweet. If you change your mind, I'll be in the back."

Mole shouted to the next dancer coming on stage. The girl came down the runway and pulled Mole on stage. Mole was dancing with the girl on stage as he started to take his shirt off. The guys around the stage handed Mole another drink, screaming for him to do more.

***

Salamor stayed in the shadows of the primate's sexual palace and admired what he had done. He would slowly kill himself by alienating all he holds true and then Salamor would push him over to his doom. The Sentry would lose her brother and he now knew where a Pure of Heart resides. That would make Vandor smile.

Chapter 9

Anne must have fallen asleep waiting for Kale. She looked at the clock and saw it was four in the morning. She glanced over at the other side of the bed and didn't see him. She got nervous. He never stayed out all night without telling her where he was. She got up and searched the house but couldn't find him. She went to call Alex but then she remembered that she changed her number. There was no way of getting ahold of her.

She was getting frantic as she didn't know what to do. It was too early to call the police. She called Dan really quick. "Sorry to wake you but have you seen Kale?"

Dan told her he went home to take Jessica on a hunting trip with his family that weekend. Anne was getting more and more nervous. The only other place she could think of checking was his dorm room. She quickly got dressed and headed out to his dorm.

***

Mole woke up to the sound of keys being rustled as some guy was calling his name. Mole just went back to bed as the smell of booze; and body odor filled the room. "Kale Moler," the man's voice said.

"Go away," Mole yelled at the door.

"Kale, it's Anne," said the voice from the other side of the door.

Mole's mind started to race. "Damn it," he said, falling out of bed. He raced to the door and opened it to find Anne standing there with the dorm manager.

"Thank you, sir," Anne said. "I'm sorry to wake you."

"No problem," the manager said. "Good luck, dude," he motioned to Mole.

Anne hugged Kale. "You had me worried sick, why didn't you..." Anne stopped. "What's that smell?" She started to look around the room. She turned on the main light to the room and Mole winced at the light shooting through his head. "Have you been drinking?"

"What?" Mole said, trying to cover his tracks.

"Kale Moler, don't you lie to me," Anne sternly said to him.

"And you don't act like my mother," he said, shutting the light off, falling back onto bed.

"I'm not, I'm concerned about you," Anne sat on Kameron's old bed.

"Nothing to be concerned about," Mole said, trying not to vomit. "Now can you please leave?"

Anne got up to the bed and turned the light on. "Kale, will you please look at me." He sat up and Anne could see shiny sparkles all over his face. "Is that glitter on your face?"

Mole checked his face with his hand and saw glitter. He was pretty much stuck in a corner and couldn't lie to get himself out of it. "I ran into a girl from school when I came into the dorm and she gave me a hug." Mole knew she didn't believe him.

"Okay Kale, if that is what you say had happened, I believe you," she said. "Now answer me this, have you been drinking?"

"Look, do you want me to take a piss test for you or something?" Kale yelled at her. "After the movie, I felt like crap with a headache, I came back here to try to get some sleep." He pulled the covers over his head. "Now can you please leave so I can get some sleep?"

"Okay, Kale," Anne got up. "Call me when you feel better." She walked to the door. "I love you."

Mole felt guilt rush over his body, "Love you too." She left and Mole was ashamed of his actions. He reached over to the corner of the bed where he had some of the bottle left. He drank a couple of swigs before trying to get back to bed.

***

Anne got coffee down the street from the house. She walked into the house to see Alex in the living room. "Alex," Anne said. "Are you okay?" She hoped Alex was here to talk.

"I'm fine," Alex said, looking around the living room. "I'm just looking for my wallet. Apparently when I got kicked out, I must have dropped it."

"Alex," Anne said. "It's on the table next to your mail."

Alex was cold to the bone as she walked past Anne. "I will get you the rent by the end of the month."

167

"Alex," Anne said, closing her eyes. She opened them to see Alex just staring at her. "Alex, I don't care about the rent. Can we talk?"

"Sure, let's talk. As long as you don't mention Gastrix or anything related to him," she demanded. "Tell me, what do you want to talk about?"

Anne wanted to tell her about Kale drinking again, but she was afraid it would lead to Gastrix and it wouldn't end well. "Alex, I just wanted you to," Anne looked at her hand holding the coffee cup. "I just wanted see if you want this coffee." She handed Alex the coffee.

"Gastrix doesn't approve of me drinking those, he wouldn't like it if it was on my breath," Alex said. "Quit trying to change me." She walked out. She turned around. "Anne."

Anne had turned around in hopes this fight would end, "Yes?"

"Call the church and tell them when you are not going to be here...I will get the rest of my stuff." Alex walked off.

***

It was late afternoon the following week after Mole lied to Anne about being at the strip club. He had stayed at his dorm room all week with just a couple of text messages back and forth from each other. It was a rough week and the only thing that got Mole through was knowing he could have drinks before starting his next day.

He wanted to relax and some of his classmates wanted to go to the strip club that he told them about. Mole thought it would be a good idea to go

168

since he needed to take his mind off of what was going on in his life. Alex had walked out of his life and he was losing Anne.

Maybe he should go see her tonight instead of going to the strip club. He looked at his phone at the last message from Anne stating, "We need to talk." He knew this was going to be some intervention or something. He texted back to her, "Come on over." He took a second to send it, but he finally hit send. Surprisingly he got a reply from her. "I will be there in 30 minutes."

Mole had enough time to hide the bottles from her as he knew whoever she was bringing to make him stop drinking would be looking for them. He just got them hidden and showered by the time Anne got to the room. He opened the door and to his surprise she was alone.

"Hey."

"Hey," she said back. "May I come in?"

He opened the door and halfway scouted to make sure there were no bottles out in the open. "What's up?"

She sat down on his bed. "Kale, you know that I love you more than anything."

Kale rolled his eyes, "Here it comes."

"Here what comes?"

"Nothing, let's just get this over with," Mole went to the bed and sat down, staring at her.

"I don't know what you are talking about, but I just wanted you to know I got accepted to a six-month paid internship at the Vatican," Anne said, showing him the acceptance letter.

Mole took the letter and read it. "How did you get this?"

"My major, apparently the school put my name into something called the Catholic Council. They want to sponsor me for a study," she said.

"When would you leave?" Mole asked her.

"End of the month," Anne said. "Not much time."

"Well, you have to take this," Mole said. "It's a chance of a lifetime."

Anne shook her head in agreement. "Yes, it is. I have to give them an answer tomorrow by five p.m. our time."

"Tell them you will go," Mole said, fighting back the tears. "Is that it?"

"Well, we are not exactly at a good place right now," she said, looking at him. "I haven't heard from you that much for about a week."

"I've been busy with school," Mole said to her. The two stared at each other. "So, what do we do about us?"

"What do you want to do?" Anne said, sitting on the bed next to him.

Mole had an urge to bend down on one knee and ask her to marry him right there.

"You will bring her down with you," the voice said. "She will resent you forever. You will ruin her life."

"Maybe we should see how it goes apart while you're away," Mole suggested.

"Is that what you want?" Anne said, wiping tears away from her face.

"I think it would be best for the both of us," Mole said.

Anne got up. "Okay." She got up from the bed and opened the door to the room. "I'll let you know when I leave."

Mole just nodded as he watched her leave.

"Ease the pain," the voice said.

Mole picked up the bottle and finished it before heading out for the night.

***

Alex sat down across from Gastrix while they were out for lunch. She started opening her mail from her old apartment. She finally got around to it since she and Gastrix have been living in a very small studio motel room. She looked through the mail and found two letters from the Catholic Council. "That's weird," Alex stared at the envelopes.

"What's up, babe?" Gastrix asked her, looking at the new phone Alex had purchased.

"This is my job," Alex said, pointing to the name on the envelope. "It's addressed to Anne."

"She's probably trying to steal your job," Gastrix said.

Alex kind of laughed, "I really don't think that."

"That arrogant skank is a manipulator," Gastrix said. "Moving out was the best thing for us."

"Anne has got one of the biggest hearts I know of," Alex said, lifting the envelope to the light. "I wonder what this is."

Gastrix grabbed the envelope and opened it. "It's a letter saying something about a Vatican study scholarship, and she is one of two finalists." He mumbled some of the other stuff he was reading when he came across, "Hey, look at this: she will be gone for six months!"

Alex grabbed the paper from his hands, "Let me see this."

Gastrix grabbed her hand and squeezed, "Don't ever do that again," he said angrily.

Komptin turned and growled at him.

"Sorry," Alex said. "Komptin, stop it." She rubbed her arm. "I just wanted to see what was going on with Anne." She continued to read. "This is going to kill Mole." She looked at the date of the letter. "This was two weeks ago; she should have found out by now." She picked up her phone to text Anne, but she remembered she took her out of her phone. "I don't know her number."

"It's a sign to cut the cord," Gastrix told her. "You are with me; you are meant to be with me." Komptin barked at him. "If I could, I would get rid of your ass too, you smelly mutt."

Alex rolled her eyes and Gastrix snapped his fingers. "Don't you roll your eyes at me either."

"I'm sorry," Alex said. "I wonder why this letter is addressed to me." She read it and Alex's face turned red. "Damn."

"What now?"

"I have a meeting with the Catholic Council tomorrow regarding revenue judgment," Alex said. "Great."

***

Mole was at the strip club with some of his classmates, drinking more than usual. "Damn

Mole, you can really drink!" one of them said, handing him another Jack and Coke.

"And pick out some strip clubs," another said. "My whole paycheck is gone, and I didn't even get it yet!"

Mole sat down at the end of the dance podium of the strip club, drinking and watching the girls walk by as he was giving them dollars. The DJ came over the loudspeaker announcing the next dancer, Pepper.

Pepper walked onto the stage, dancing as the guys went crazy. Mole looked at the girl and he knew that he had seen her before. He just couldn't place it. The girl walked up to him and waved like she knew him. The guys were throwing all their money at her as she stepped around all of them. She laid down on the floor and wrapped her arms around Mole. "I'm glad you're here."

Mole had to do a double-take. "You're that girl from the hallway."

She looked at him, "You know it." She put a dollar between his ear and head like a pencil and licked his ear as she grabbed it. "Meet me at the bar after my dance."

"I'll be there," Mole said, finishing his drink.

After the song, Mole went to the bar and waited for Pepper to join him. He motioned for the bartender for one more.

"Hey, man, I think you've had enough," the bartender said, taking his glass.

"Oh, come on, Phil, he can handle it," Pepper said, putting her hand on top of Mole's.

"Thanks," Mole said.

"I'm Sharon, but my stage name is Pepper," she said. She playfully ran the tip of her fingernails on top of Mole's hand.

"Kale, my stage name is Mole," Mole joked as he took the drink the bartender reluctantly gave him.

"Can I tell you a secret, Mole?" Sharon smirked.

"What's that?" He turned to her.

"I've had my eye on you since the first time we crossed paths in the hallway," Sharon said. "And it just so happened that your friends bought you a private dance." She leaned into him. "It will be something you will never forget."

"I really shouldn't," Mole admitted.

"Why? Do you have a girlfriend?" she asked.

Mole looked down at his drink, "No, I guess I don't."

"Good," she grabbed his hand and walked him to the dance room.

Mole sat down on the couch, looking up at her. "What do I do?

"You've never had a lap dance?" she asked out of amazement.

"Honestly, no."

"Well, I'm going to have to make this extra special," she said as she sat next to him, playing with his hair.

The music started so that was her cue to stand up. She leaned over Mole. She turned around to sit on his lap and moved to the music. She turned back around, putting her arms around Kale's neck. Mole reached over to the table next to him and grabbed a flower. "Can you put this on the right side of your hair," he asked.

"That's a first," Sharon said, grinding away on Mole's lap. She got off his lap when the song ended. She stared at him and then she pulled him off the couch. "Here's another secret, Mole," she said. "There's another room in the back." Sharon looked at him. "I'm just going to say this bluntly, I'm going to see if it's open. You and me in that room, we are going to make something special happen."

The song was over, and Mole got up. "When?"

"I just need to make sure no one else is using it," Sharon said. "You are going to have one hell of a night."

Mole walked out of the room and sat back down on the bar, motioning for another drink. The bartender gave him the drink and he started to drink it. He looked over at Sharon talking to the other dancers pointing at Mole. There was no doubt of what would happen if Mole went into that back room. Mole sat and stared at the drink, debating if he should go back there.

"I thought you couldn't drink," a voice from behind him said.

Mole turned around and saw Kameron there looking at him. "Kameron, what are you doing here?"

"Some classmates of mine said to meet them here to celebrate my graduation. I had a break in between training, so I thought I would drive up and join them," Kameron looked around. "Where's Anne?"

"Anne and I are over," he said, slurring his words.

"I'm sorry to hear that," Kameron said. "Do you think you should be drinking? No offense, but I thought you were a recovering alcoholic."

"Over three years," Mole admitted, falling off the barstool. Kameron caught him before he fell to the ground.

"Come on, big guy," Kameron said. "I think you've had enough."

"Hey, he's coming with me," Sharon said.

Kameron turned around as he was trying to hold Mole up.

"Kameron!" She hugged him. "Oh my God, I thought you left."

"I did," he said. "But I've got to get my friend here to a little meeting."

"Call me," Sharon said to him.

"Have a good night, Sharon," Kameron said, carrying Mole out the door. "Geez, you're heavy." Kameron carried him over to his car and laid Mole in the backseat. He picked up his phone, hoping he still had Anne's number.

***

Sanah decided to go for a walk before heading out to find more to infiltrate. It felt good not to have to hunt on his walks. Plus, he knew that infiltrators were nearby and that he could call them at a moment's notice. It really felt good to have the power of knowing you are successful.

The park was empty this late at night. Sanah looked up to the sky and saw the lite forces of the entire past angel warriors that had died. He did notice a strange purple one that stood out among the others. He could only figure that he was Alex's former mentor.

Sanah strolled out of the park and ran into a beautiful blonde woman with two other girls at her side. "Sanah," she said to him.

This was the moment he thought could end this war. This opportunity would not present itself again. "Celestial," he bowed. It took every effort not to stab her right then and there, but there was something he needed to know.

"I heard you were in the area," she said, looking over his shoulders. "How have you been? I am truly sorry for your loss."

Sanah just nodded at her. "Surprised to see you here."

"Oh, why is that?" she asked, as she started to walk with him in the peaceful park.

"Just not your type of town," he stated

"I like to check up on the newest Lite Sentry from time to time," Celestial said. "There has not been an infiltrator sighting in the Holy Land for quite some time, is this why you have come to the States?"

"It is," Sanah confirmed. "I don't know why you are taking an interest in her. She is a self-centered, undisciplined, harlot."

"She has a lot to learn, but she is full of potential. Her power is not as matched as yours though, but putting you two together in the same town will have the Dark scattering," Celestial stated. "We must watch the balance. Neither side should escalate."

"They seem to be still sticking around, my queen," Sanah pointed out. He looked back at

Celestial's bodyguards who were keeping a close eye on him. Sanah knew that look they were giving him. They did not trust him and could tell they were on high alert. "Before you leave, may I ask you something?"

"Of course," Celestial told him. "You can ask me anything."

"Can you see if my wife and son are okay?" Sanah asked of her.

Celestial closed her eyes. A faint gold glow could be seen under her eyelids, "They are at peace, but sad."

"Okay, just what I wanted to know," Sanah said, lighting his purple fists. He went to strike Celestial but before that happened, he felt a Lite Spear jab into his shoulder. He managed to swing as he fell down, cutting Celestial's side open. She fell to the ground as liquid gold lite dropped from the wound. She cried in pain as she crawled to lean against a building wall.

Sanah grabbed the Lite Bow and swung Devine into the brick wall. Sanah went to punch Devine but she quickly moved out of the way. He managed to kick her as she dropped. Sanah punched her on the side of the head, knocking her to the ground. Sanah turned his attention to Ariel who was keeping guard on Celestial as she was on her hands and knees, bleeding. He formed a spear and swung but was blocked by Ariel's Lite Sword. Ariel punched Sanah in the stomach as Devine went to stab him from behind. Sanah moved out of the way. He spun around as he elbowed Devine in the back of the head. Devine fell into Ariel's arms. The two of them regained their fighting stances as Sanah stared with hate.

Sanah took in a deep breath as he walked up to them. He formed a spear as Devine and Ariel cracked their necks as he attacked. The three of them dodged and blocked each other's attacks. The Guardians received some hits, so did Sanah. Ariel suddenly spun and sliced Sanah's leg from behind as Devine hit him in the chest, knocking him to the ground. The two of them were about to strike when they saw Celestial, gaining their attention. Sanah shot a Lite Beam into Ariel, throwing her into Devine, knocking them both against a brick wall. They fell to the ground a with painful groan. Ariel checked her lip as neon blue liquid blood dropped onto the ground where she stood with Devine who refused to wipe her blood dripping from her nose. They turned around to the sound of infiltrators coming from the shadows and the fire escapes. Sanah used this distraction to escape from the Conduit's bodyguards.

The purple haired bodyguard stood in a defensive stance position overlooking the situation while the green one tended to Celestial as she held her wound.

"We need to get to a doorway," the green one said. "She is cut deep."

"Take her, I will give you the time," the purple one said as she watched Sanah escape into the darkness of the alley. Multiple infiltrators' eyes appeared around them.

"Alexandria is nearby, Komptin should lead her this way," Celestial told them as she was covering her wound.

The infiltrators slowly came out from the darkness, growling and hissing towards the three Lite Beings.

"This is going to suck," the three of them said.

***

"Komptin, stop it," Alex said, pulling on the leash. "We are going this way." She knew he was on edge ever since she felt the stale air from the infiltrators taking advantage of someone's submission.

"What's with your dog?" Gastrix asked. "He's becoming a lot more trouble than he's worth."

"He's just antsy because our walks have been kind of short to nonexistent lately," Alex commented. "I really should take him for a long walk tonight," she said, bending over and petting Komptin. "Settle down." Komptin just looked at her and flashed his eyes.

"Put a muzzle on that mutt," Gastrix said as he was staring at his phone. "Why don't you just get rid of that dog?"

Komptin turned to look at Gastrix. Alex almost thought he understood what he said. "I'd get rid of you before I get rid of him," Alex said, still petting him.

Gastrix turned and pushed Alex over and she landed on her back. Komptin snapped at him with a vicious bark. "Don't you ever put me below anything else." He started getting mad. "No one will love you more than I do. You are a smart-ass, witch-looking, goth chick which no one else will love." Komptin stood between Alex and Gastrix.

Alex wiped off her tears from being yelled at and regained her composure. She got up and fixed her new hairdo, which she genuinely hated. "I'm sorry, but don't push me."

Gastrix slapped her across the face as hard as he could, catching Alex off guard as she fell back to the ground. "You don't tell me what to do. I know what's best for you. You are nothing without me," Gastrix threw his hands up and walked away from Alex and Komptin. "I don't know how your dumbass will ever learn."

Komptin morphed into his fighting form and growled with continuous blue glowing eyes. Alex jumped up and stood in front of her protector. "No!" Komptin started walking towards Gastrix in a hunting formation as if he were going to pounce. Alex pushed back on his head as her feet were sliding on the ground. Komptin broke free of her grip and headed towards Gastrix. Alex didn't have a choice. Alex shot a Lite Beam at her companion that pushed Komptin into the wall with her blast. She knew it didn't hurt him, but he got the point. He morphed back down to his dog form and went back to Alex's side. Alex didn't know if she hurt his ego or feelings, but Komptin refused to look at her as she went chasing Gastrix down, apologizing.

***

Ariel was continuing to fend off the attacks as Devine carried Celestial to the nearby church. As both the infiltrators and Lite beings knew, they would be in safe haven once they reached the first step of a cathedral.

A glowing lite kept on pouring out of Celestial as she tried to handle her own weight to help Devine carry her to safety. One infiltrator managed to swipe at Celestial from a nearby road crossing, but she managed to block the attack, using her back.

Ariel distinguished the beast immediately once she saw her friend in protection get injured. They managed to get close to a church as they only had to cross the street to get to sacred grounds. The only obstacle were two infiltrators standing in their path. They started to charge when Devine threw her Lite Spear at one, knocking them in the chest and falling to the ground. The other lunged as Ariel sliced its head with her sword. The path was clear.

They made their way across the street as another infiltrator charged out from behind a parked car. "Forgive me, my lady," Ariel said as she struggled to pick up Celestial and throw her with all her might onto the steps of the church. The infiltrator jumped at Ariel who knew she was about to join her brother and sisters in the stars. Devine interrupted the lunge by picking up her spear sticking out of the chest of the infiltrator before it disappeared and jabbed it through the neck of the attacking infiltrator. It howled before disappearing into the night.

Ariel and Devine crawled on their hands and knees onto the church steps, joining Celestial. Sanah appeared, holding his wound, staring at them.

"Why?" Celestial asked, trying to fathom what had just happened.

Sanah looked at her with pure hate. He flashed his purple eyes and turned around, walking into the darkness with the remaining infiltrators as the sun came up in the distance.

***

Anne found herself up all night crying, wearing the sweatshirt that Kale gave her. Even though they grew up and went to school all through kindergarten to graduation, she never really knew him until that night at the lake beach. She tried everything to keep warm, but she was shivering cold to the bone. She couldn't get past how bad things got so fast.

She had been with him for over three years and it was going so well. This all started when Gastrix got Kale drunk that night without him knowing. She should have stayed by his side to make sure he wasn't drinking. She should have been there for him.

"You failed this relationship," a voice from the dark echoed through her mind.

Anne looked around to see where that was coming from, "Who's there?"

"You are the reason he's drinking again," the voice insinuated.

Anne got out of bed and grabbed her crucifix around her neck. She ran over to her dresser and found a Bible. She opened it up, "I have something to tell you, 'Second Timothy Chapter 4 Verse 18: and the Lord shall deliver me from every evil work and will preserve me unto his heavenly kingdom: to whom be glory forever and ever'." Anne looked in the corner where the voice was coming, "So get the hell out of my apartment."

Anne then saw a set of glowing red eyes coming from the corner in a shadowy mist. It started floating towards her. She stood her grounds, staring right at the creature. "You can go now," she calmly told the monster.

The floating creature struggled to reach her but was forcefully pulled back out of the apartment, vanishing into the sunlight peering up to start the day. Anne closed her eyes and thanked God for her protection. She was interrupted by the sound of her phone ringing. "Hello," Anne said. "No, you didn't wake me, is everything all right?"

It was Kameron who called to tell Anne that Kale was in a hotel room over on the other side of town. "He's passed out on the bed," he continued to say. "I think he's in a lot of pain."

"Did he get hurt?" Anne's heart stopped. "Is he okay?"

"He's not physically hurt, but I think you need to talk to him," Kameron said.

"I'm leaving now. I will be there as soon as possible," Anne said. "Please text me the address. Thank you, Kameron," Anne hung up the phone. She looked on the side of her phone to see that it was put on silent. "How'd the phone ring?" Anne looked to the sun peeking out between the buildings. She smiled and said, "Thank you."

***

Alex snuck out of bed while Gastrix was still sleeping. She didn't really like lying in bed wide-awake while he slept, but he liked having her next to him. Alex looked in the mirror and stared at herself. She hated her hair. It was only down to her shoulders and bright red. She only did this because Gastrix had wanted her to dress more cybergoth so she wouldn't be an embarrassment to their friends.

She put her dark eyeliner on and her white skull shirt. She looked around for her black skirt but couldn't find it. She did find some bright red pants that Gastrix told her to buy. She put them on and looked in the mirror. She didn't care for them. She took them off and threw them in the closet. She did happen to find an old pair of black stretch pants she hadn't worn since the battle where Osiah and Sara were killed. She looked out the window and saw the purple star through the morning sun.

Alex put on the pants and a grey skirt she had buried in a closet. She looked to the floor of the bed and Komptin wasn't to be found. She looked around the tiny little studio apartment which had clothes, dishes, food containers piled everywhere. She saw Komptin looking out the window in the sunlight. She approached to pet him, but he pulled away and sat next to the door. "What's the matter?" she asked him. He looked at her and then turned his head to the side. He laid his head on the floor and shut his eyes.

"Where are you off to?" Gastrix said, walking around in nothing but a pair of shorts.

"I have my meeting with the church this morning," Alex reminded him.

"You need to quit that job," Gastrix said. "You could find a different one."

"There's only one other company that I know of that is interested, and the benefits are not that great," Alex pointed out. She looked at herself in the mirror with disgust. She didn't like the way she looked. Then Gastrix came up behind her, moving his hands up her shirt. "Stop it!"

"Come on," Gastrix said. "It will help you relax."

"No," Alex said, slapping his hands away.

"Don't tell me no," Gastrix said, grabbing her by the arms. He threw her on the bed.

"I said no," Alex said. Gastrix held her down and Alex refused to kiss him. Gastrix was getting mad at Alex's refusal and started to rip her shirt, exposing her bra. "Stop it." Alex felt her arms start to pulsate but controlled it as she easily pushed him off of her.

He got up. "Fine, but I'm coming to that meeting with you," Gastrix said, getting dressed. "I don't want them filling your head up with lies and all that bull."

"Fine," Alex said in agreement just so she could get going. She looked to Komptin who turned further away from the two of them. "Come on, Komptin," she grabbed his leash. "We gotta go."

***

Anne walked into the hotel room half expecting to see something which would change the course of the relationship forever. She knocked on the door, imagining seeing some evidence of Kale and another girl in the room. Even though she knew Kameron got the room, she was worried some other girl was going to be in there with him.

186

Kameron opened the door, still in the clothes he must have worn last night. She looked and saw Kale in bed, looking like death had rolled over him with a steam roller. "How is he?"

"The booze is pretty much worn off," Kameron said, rubbing the back of his neck. Anne pretty much thought he slept in the chair. "He's going to have one hell of a hangover, though."

"Thank you for this," Anne said.

"The room is paid for," Kameron said as he grabbed a water bottle.

"Let me pay you for it," Anne suggested, opening her purse.

Kameron put his massive, gentle hands on top of her hands on the purse, "No. Don't worry about that." He looked at Kale who was just rubbing his eyes, looking at Anne and Kameron staring at him.

"Anne?" Kale asked looking at them. He then turned to the side of the bed and puked.

***

Alex got to the church and came up through the basement of the back door. She could hear some people talking down in one of the rooms. Gastrix was walking behind her, listening to music and Komptin walked ahead of her, no doubt heading for the main worship room. She walked as she saw a sign for an Alcoholic Anonymous meeting being conducted. She tried sneaking by, but something had caught her eye. She recognized one of the people in the meeting. "Mole?" she softly said. She watched as one of the leaders of the group

187

asked, "Is there anything that someone would like to say this morning?"

She watched Mole raise his hands. She had never seen him so vulnerable before. He got up to the podium and she stayed out of view so he couldn't see her. "My name is Kale—most call me Mole—and I'm an alcoholic."

The group simultaneously said, "Hi, Mole."

Mole just stared at the group before the leader of the group spoke up, "It's okay, son, you can take your time."

"When I was in high school, I drank a lot…I mean a lot," he started off. "I used to hide it in my school locker, mixed the perfect amount of vodka and orange juice not to get caught, and I found myself naked on the football field once not remembering how I got there," he chuckled. "Then one drunken night I stole a car from a man's garage and ran into his tree." Mole looked out the basement window at the sun. "Long story short, the prosecuting attorney, who turned out to be my father, sent me to juvey for four months. One of the best things that ever happened to me. Three of the best things that ever happened to me was a result of that. I got a wonderful parole officer, who was more of a mentor to me, who helped me achieve an Iron Man race when I turned 18. Second best thing was that I found out my best friend, who I loved like a sister, was actually my sister."

Alex had a flashback to that night at the pizza parlor when they found out they were actually brother and sister. The thought was interrupted by Gastrix, "I gotta piss." He left for the bathroom.

"But it seems like life kept taking things away from me. My outlet to combat the temptation to booze was taken away from me when I got jumped by a maniac who left me for dead. All I really remember was a purple dog and …." Mole started to trail off. "Now I'm injured because I cannot run, swim, or bike. On top of that, my mentor died just prior to my race that we trained so hard for," Mole was starting to wipe the tears from his face. "Then one night, somebody spiked my Cokes with vodka." Mole looked down at his feet. "To this day, I will say I didn't taste the booze or maybe I subconsciously blocked it out, but all I know it led to the destruction of the one thing that was most important to me." Mole stared at the audience, "I'm not going to say, 'I loved' her because that is a lie; I love her, I love her more than anything, but the booze and my weakness to handle it pushed her away and I'm afraid I lost her forever."

"They broke up," Alex whispered to herself. She got a sour lump in her stomach as she felt as if she was going to be sick. "Oh God, Mole, Anne, why didn't you call?" And then she remembered she had gotten a new phone number and didn't bother to tell them. Alex felt ashamed as she turned around to see Anne staring at her holding a cup of coffee.

"What are you doing here?" Anne asked out of disappointment.

"I have a meeting with the Council," Alex answered. "Don't know why they came from D.C. to talk to me."

Anne stood there watching Alex, "Maybe they had other business here as well."

"Anne," Alex said. "I didn't know Mole. I didn't know that…"

"Stop," she held out her hand. "How could you? You left. You left us. You completely shut us out of your life. And for what?"

Just then, Gastrix came out of the bathroom. He saw Alex talking to Anne and came over, putting his arm around her neck tightly. "The stuck-up snob."

Anne just rolled her eyes at Gastrix and looked back at Alex. "I guess I got my answer." She started walking down the hall to the church library but stopped herself to turn around to Alex, "If you have any feelings left for us, for him, you will make sure he doesn't see you here." She turned back around to walk into the library muttering, "You've caused enough damage to him."

Alex felt shame. Somehow, she knew the last time she saw Mole on the street that day was the day he started drinking again. She knew it was her actions that night that probably pushed him over the edge. She started to walk towards Anne but was stopped by noticing the clock on the wall. She was already late for her appointment. She couldn't do anything right.

"What a snob," Gastrix said to Alex, putting his headphones back on.

"Far from it," Alex softly said. She turned around and headed up to meet the Council.

***

Alex felt like she was in high school getting in trouble with the school board. She sat on the other

190

end of the table. The Cardinal was on the other end with one other young-looking priest to his right. The Cardinal sat and stared at her while the young priest was listing all the purchases on her credit card bill. Alex was getting embarrassed, especially when the charges at "JJ's House of Exotic Pleasure" were announced.

"Ms. Johnson, is there something more interesting outside than your blatant disregard of policy?" the young priest yelled.

"That's enough, Father Tom," the Cardinal said calmly, closing his eyes with his hands folded "Anything else?"

Alex looked up at the young priest. So that is who Father Tom was. That was who she had been reporting to. She couldn't tell that much about him, but she knew one thing: she didn't make a good first impression.

Father Tom continued, "We also have reports that no hunts have taken place for quite some time and there was Infiltration and then we have what happened last night."

Alex's attention peaked, "What happened last night?"

Father Tom quickly turned to her, "Who do you think you are, asking such a question after your behavior? You should have been there. You were just down a couple of blocks!"

"Father, please," the Cardinal said. He looked over to a man in a suit with an earpiece. "Tony," he called to him. He motioned for him and whispered something in his ear. The man nodded and left the room. Father Tom stared at her and shook his head from disbelief in Alex. Alex couldn't look him in the eye. The Cardinal just stared at her, no anger, no disappointment. It was concern.

Alex looked around the room for some sort of familiarity. Something that would make her feel at ease. Not even Komptin came into the meeting room with her. The only thing she knew was that Gastrix was sitting outside the room, pissed because he had to wait in the lobby. She turned back to look at the Cardinal who was still looking at her with no expression. The only thing he was doing was tapping his finger quietly on the table. He was no doubt contemplating his next actions.

It seemed like an eternity before something was said. "Here's a shocker," the Cardinal said to Alex, breaking the silence. "I don't have any kids."

Alex caught herself fighting a smile.

"I know, right," the elderly man said, getting up. "A man of cloth for over fifty years with no children. Your mind is blown, isn't it?"

Alex looked down at her feet. She could not bring herself to look at the man. The Cardinal walked to a couch next to the window to sit down. "Please, join me, Alex." He motioned for her to sit down next to him. Alex moved over to him. The warmth of the sun felt good, but she was also shivering from being cold for some reason. Father Tom just stayed at the table, reading a transcript of some sorts.

"But here is something you may not know," the Cardinal continued. "I have seen more troubled teens and young adults come across my parishes more times than I can count. I can tell the signs of someone in trouble a mile away."

Alex looked up, fighting a lump in the back of her throat. "I feel like I'm falling; and it won't stop. All my support branches are breaking, sending me farther down the dark hole, and I'm afraid at what is at the bottom," she trembled. "I feel so cold and lonely."

He put his hand on her shoulders. "Sometimes, a single gesture is all you need to start your way back to being you." The man in the suit came back in and handed the Cardinal a brown paper bag. "Thank you," the Cardinal told the man. The Cardinal stuck his hand in the brown paper bag and pulled out an Apollo Energy Drink and handed it to Alex.

Alex laughed as she stared at it before opening it. She took a drink, "That's good. How'd you know?"

"Father Joe said it was your favorite," the Cardinal stated.

Alex smiled at the thought of Father Joe, which led to her thinking of Osiah, then Sara, and then losing Mole and Anne as well because of her, "Oh Father Joe, how is he?"

"He's doing well," the Cardinal said.

"How much trouble am I in?" Alex asked, barely able to look at him. She could see Father Tom lifting his head from the paper he was reading to see what the Cardinal was going to say.

"Don't worry about the revenue report. Let's just say you have used your only get out jail free card." His caring smile made Alex feel as if she wished she could never leave the moment.

"Thank you," she said, sniffing in the snot that was forming. "And I promise to start back on my hunts again. I will find the infiltrated and dispose of them."

"Well, we have something else we may need to show you," The Cardinal motioned to Father Tom.

Alex turned around to see Celestial enter the room bandaged with a glowing liquid oozing out of it. "Celestial!" Alex came running towards her, bowing before giving her a hug. Celestial winced in pain "What happened?"

"I will tell you what happened," Ariel spoke up, stepping towards Alex.

"Your actions caused this," Devine continued, stepping in between Alex and Celestial.

"Ariel, Devine, please," Celestial said, putting her hands on the two of them. The two of them stepped back behind Celestial. She turned to the Cardinal. "Thank you, Frank."

"Not a problem, my lady," he motioned for the young priest and man with a suit to join him out of the room. "I'm hungry, how about a burger?" The two of them agreed as they left the room.

Alex turned her attention back to a wounded Celestial, "What happened?"

"We have lost a Lite Sentry," Celestial sadly stated.

"Sanah?" Alex asked. "He was so powerful and skilled."

"And still is," Ariel and Devine both said. They seemed to have a look of disappointment in themselves for allowing the Conduit to get injured.

Alex looked at the both of them, "You mean?"

"Yes, he has turned to the Dark. He has got much pain and hate in him," Celestial said.

Alex turned her back away from the three of them. "I've been so preoccupied I didn't see this coming. This has been happening a lot lately."

"Come with me," Celestial said, holding out her hand. Alex accepted as they walked out of the room where Gastrix followed them.

Ariel and Devine ensured he stayed behind them as they walked up to the worship room where Komptin came running up to Celestial, licking her face. "I am okay, Komptin."

"Good, you can have that goddamn mutt," Gastrix said.

Ariel and Devine turned around to Gastrix whispering, "Language."

"What? This is all made up bull anyway. Come on, Alex, let's get out of here," he made his way up to Celestial and grabbed Alex's hand.

"You look tired," Celestial said to Gastrix as he fell asleep. He fell backwards as Ariel and Devine caught him, placing him on a church bench.

"I thought we had no power here? It was a safe zone," Alex asked, watching him being gently placed on the church pew.

"He is completely safe," Celestial said. "In fact, he is going to have the best sleep of his life."

"I need to extinguish Sanah, don't I?" Alex asked, looking at Gastrix sleeping on the bench.

"No Lite Sentry has ever fought another," Celestial pointed out. "It will not be easy. He is also planning something if he is helping with Infiltration. It would be beneficial to find out what."

"I will go tonight," Alex said.

"You are not ready," Celestial said. "You need to have a clear head and strong heart if you are to survive."

"I'm good," Alex said, not being able to look her in the eyes.

"Really?" Celestial pointed to Anne and Mole walking out of the church.

Alex noted that the two of them were not holding hands or walking close to each other. "They want nothing to do with me." Alex turned around Celestial, "I really messed this one up to a massive pile of crap. I just don't know why."

Celestial winced in pain as she held her side. She had glowing blood on her hand as she touched Alex's cheeks. Celestial's blood seemed to disappear when Alex leaned into her hand and a feeling of warmth filled her body. "Have a sip of your drink," Celestial suggested.

"Gastrix doesn't like me to drink this. He's going to be mad I had a couple of sips of this already," Alex pointed out as she stared at the can. She looked back at him passed out on the pew. "If he wakes up and sees me drinking this, he's going to be pissed."

"I have to go," Celestial said, forcing a caring smile but from what Alex could tell, she was worried for Alex. She walked towards the staircase to the church tower. She turned to Ariel and Devine. "Will you be coming?"

"We will be right behind you, my lady," Devine said.

"We have a mess to pick up," Ariel stated.

Alex watched Celestial walk upstairs and disappear. Then Alex felt two hands slap her on the back of the head. "What in Heaven is wrong with you?" Ariel and Devine asked out of disbelief they were asking this question.

Chapter 10

Mole didn't really say anything in the car. Anne kept the radio off and just drove; quietly. The sun beaming in the car just emphasized her beauty and innocence. He wanted to tell her that nothing happened at the strip club, but he was confused because he didn't know where they were in their relationship.

"Anne," Mole managed to say, not being able to look at her.

"Yes, Kale," Anne said, continuing to drive.

"I just, well, I just wanna say thank you," He managed to say. "You didn't have to come."

"Kale, there is a difference between having to help someone and wanting to," she told him.

Mole looked out the window at a young couple holding hands while they were at a stop light. "And which one was the reason you came this morning; having or wanting?"

Anne looked to Mole who was awaiting an answer, "What do you think?"

Mole actually didn't know the answer to the question, "Where are we going?"

"Back to your dorm room."

Mole thought those were the words of doom. "Oh, okay."

"Why?" Anne turned her head to Kale. "Did you have somewhere else you'd rather be?"

"Anne, I," Mole said, trying to get it out but stopped himself to stare out the window. "Nothing."

"Kale, I'm not going through this again like we did in high school where either of us were too scared to tell each other how we feel or want, so I'm just going to tell you," Anne flat out said.

"No, I'm going to do it, because if you say it first then I don't want you to think it was just a reaction to what you said," Kale said.

"What?" Anne asked in confusion.

"Damn it, Anne, I love you. I love you more than anything I know. I have never been so lost and because of my problem with booze I drove you out of my life and it is tearing me up inside. Losing you is the worst thing that has ever happened to me and I'm counting the night Roger kicked the living crap out of me," Kale pleaded. "I will never forgive myself for putting you through this. I truly am sorry. I hope someday we can be friends again."

Anne quickly turned into a parking lot of a restaurant and turned to Kale after slamming on the brakes. "No."

Mole stomach dropped "I understand."

"Kale, you don't," Anne informed him. "I love you more than anything. I'm saying I don't want to break up. Every relationship has its rough times. I'm going to be there for you to get you back on sobriety and somehow get Alex back in our lives." Anne placed her hands on Kale's face. She pulled him in for a kiss. "I'm not going to leave you."

"I love you so much," Kale said, returning her kiss. He looked at her passionately and said with confidence, "I want you to go to the Vatican. It's only six months; it's the length of only one Iron Man training plan. We'll be fine."

"What about getting your sobriety back?" Anne asked out of concern.

Kale laughed, "You know, honestly, I know I'll be okay. Just knowing I'm not losing you, is all I need. For the first time in quite a while, I feel no pain."

Anne started to cry, "I love you, Kale." The two had started kissing when they were interrupted by a police car behind them with their lights on.

***

"Hey, that hurt!" Alex said to Ariel and Devine who were standing on either side of her. "What was that for?" Alex started to rub the back of her head while creating some distance between them.

"Do you think we are stupid?" Ariel asked Alex out of anger. Alex's nerves shot up from seeing the faces of determination on the Conduit Guardians. The two angels confidently walked in her direction.

"Do you think we do not know what is happening?" Devine interjected with the same annoyance. The two of them stared at Alex as they continued walking towards her.

Alex turned around and walked between the church pews on the other side of the aisle from Gastrix who was still passed out from Celestial. "What are you talking about?"

"The marks on your body," Devine flew over the pews, landing next to Alex.

"They may be faint, but we do see them," Ariel pointed out as she joined Devine on the other side of Alex. Komptin followed Ariel and Devine with his glowing blue eyes. He growled and barked out loud.

"He can't hurt me," Alex pointed out. "I've gotten hit a lot worse than what he can ever do to me."

"Really? Do you hear yourself?" Devine was shocked at Alex's answer.

"You are actually accepting him striking you?" Ariel pointed to multiple places on Alex's face where Gastrix had hit her.

Both of them harshly said," "Do you think abuse is purely physical pain?"

"Shut up, what do you know? You don't know anything about love," Alex said. "Komptin, watch Gastrix, I'm going to go get the car." Alex stormed out of the church. Thunder and lightning came across the sky as Devine and Ariel dropped in front of Alex. She turned around to see Komptin in his gargoyle state breathing heavily with his eyes glowing.

Devine grabbed Alex and spun her around, "You think what you are in is love?"

Ariel pointed her finger right in Alex's face "You are telling us you enjoy what he does to you?" Alex got frustrated and forcefully walked in between the two angels to get across the street. She got to her car which had a parking ticket on the windshield. "Just great." She put the ticket in her purse. She turned around to have Ariel in full body armor, displaying her misty wings and halo, grab her by the neck and lifted her up by the throat.

"So, you really think abuse is love?" Ariel asked her.

"You truly are a stupid primate," Devine stated.

"I bet you even let him hurt the people you really do love," Ariel continued their rant.

Devine immediately added on, "Some protector you are."

Alex got thrown through the window to the store on the sidewalk. It was an empty office space available for rent. Alex had a feeling it was going to be renovated after this talk. Alex grabbed her throat, trying to ease the pain. Devine walked up to her and pushed her down with her foot. "Stay down there since that is where you belong."

Ariel confidently walked up to her to join Devine. The two angels kept their feet on Alex, not letting her up. "You are as blind as you are dumb," Ariel added.

"Stop it, you have no idea. He is the only one who will love me." She lit her fist and broke free of her grip. Her eyes flashed blue as she clenched her teeth, staring at the two angels in a fighting position.

"Really?" The two warrior angels both said as they stared at her in disbelief.

Devine asked her, "You really want to do this?"

"Little pathetic human," Ariel gave the final insult.

Alex screamed and attacked the two of them. She swung at Devine who easily dodged the punch and pushed her in the back, smashing her head into the drywall, causing debris to fall on her. Alex's eyes flashed and she attacked, swinging at Ariel who kicked her in the stomach. She grabbed Alex's arm and swung her through a wall, causing her to land on her back in the next room over.

The two of them calmly looked over Alex without saying a word. Their arrogance just infuriated Alex more as she screamed at them. Ariel stepped to the side, tripping Alex into the air as Devine caught Alex mid-flight into a headlock. Alex was trying to break free, but she lost her strength as Devine slowly cut off her air supply. Alex's fist stopped glowing as Devine dropped her to the ground.

"You are nothing," Ariel told her.

"Pitiful, actually," Devine corrected her as she let Alex go, pushing her into the wall.

The two of them looked at each other, "Vandor's feces is actually better than this thing."

Alex screamed as she got up and attacked them. She charged them and they both simultaneously grabbed her arms and dropped her to the ground, placing their knees on her back. "You don't touch or talk to me like that!"

"THEN WHY DO YOU LET HIM DO THAT TO YOU!" both yelled at the same time.

Alex started to cry as her body went limp. Ariel and Devine took a moment to look at each other before gently lifting her onto her knees. Alex sat down on the floor, crying. The two angels stood in front of her. "I thought I was just doing what needed to be done for love." Alex continued to cry into her shirt. "I thought I was doing what needed to be done." She started wiping her nose from the snot and the tears from her eyes. "I see it all the time. All around me, people in relationships. It's like something I can't have."

"What is that?" Devine knelt down next to Alex, placing her hand on Alex's knee and the other on her shoulder.

"What is it that you cannot have?" Ariel probed, joining her partner next to Alex, putting her hands-on Alex's opposite knee in the same places as Devine.

"I can't love, I never have. I thought I just had to settle. I thought something was wrong with me. I don't deserve love if I can't return it. What's wrong with me?" Alex pleaded to Ariel and Devine.

They both placed their arms and wings around Alex as she continued to cry, giving a welcoming comfort to the Lite Sentry. "Nothing is wrong with you, Alexandria," Devine said stroking her hair.

"Well," Ariel pinched Alex's hair. "Maybe your new hairdo."

Alex laughed in between her tears. "I have nothing left. I lost everyone," Alex said, holding onto their arms, shivering as they held onto her.

"I would not say that," the two of them said.

Alex felt Komptin come up to her and lick her face. She felt Ariel and Devine let her go so she could hug Komptin. "I'm so sorry, boy. I'm so sorry." She continued to hug Komptin as he snuggled up to her for affection. Ariel and Devine got up helping Alex get up as well. The three of them, along with Komptin, looked over the mess they created. "Do you think the owner will notice that we were here?" Alex sniffled. Then a light fixture dropped as Alex could have sworn both Ariel and Devine gave a somewhat smile.

***

"I can't believe he gave us a ticket," Kale said to Anne as they entered the apartment.

"I can't believe you said, 'but officer, we have love' as an excuse," Anne laughed putting down her keys on the table next to the door.

Kale grabbed her wrist and swung her around, dipping her into a makeshift dance, "But it was the truth." He kissed her and guided her onto the floor. She started to unbutton his shirt as she laid on the floor. "Here?" Kale asked. "What if Brenda walks in?"

"Well, then you better hurry," Anne said, smiling.

Kale got up and took his jacket and shirt off and took off his pants rather quickly. He was wearing nothing but his socks as he was seductively dancing for Anne as she remained on the floor, laughing.

"Oh my God!" Alex said upon walking into the apartment.

"Alex," Anne said, crab crawling from underneath Kale to stand up.

"What are you doing here?" Kale asked, standing in the living room, refusing to cover himself up.

Alex held up her hand so she wouldn't have to see Little Mole. "I just wanted to say," she adjusted her hand and still looked away, "I just came here to…" She tried saying again. "Mole, can you put that thing away?"

"No," Kale said with his arms folded, facing her. "What do you want, Alex?"

"Kale," Anne said, grabbing his bathrobe from the bathroom. She threw it at him. "Come on, no sister should have to see her brother's little buddy."

"Well, I had this whole thing planned in my head but for some reason I lost my train of thought," she admitted.

"Well thanks, Alex! That clears everything up," Kale said, going onto the couch. He picked up the remote to look at the broken TV. "Oh yeah, our TV is busted." He just tossed the remote backwards and Alex instinctively caught it with ease.

"Damn it, Mole, I'm trying to apologize," Alex said to him. Komptin came in the door and jumped onto his favorite chair.

"Yeah, for what?" Mole got up from the couch. "For your boyfriend getting me trashed, for him breaking the TV? What, Alex, what the hell are you apologizing for?"

Alex had tears running down her eyes, "I'm sorry for not listening to you. To either of you."

Mole had a sudden rush of guilt from making his sister cry in front of him. Anne and Kale looked at each other. Anne was waiting for Kale's reaction. Kale looked at his sister, studying her. He looked over at his emotionally torn up sister, "Order pizza tonight and we'll call it even."

The three of them hugged each other.

***

Sanah went into the abandoned hospital where the infiltrators seemed to reside. He sat down on an old recliner, watching the infiltrators fight over scraps of pieces of what he could only see was the body of a young college student.

"You look upset," Salamor was mystified before him.

206

"I almost ended this war," Sanah said. "I wounded her, I wounded her badly."

"Not many got so close," the dark figure said.

Sanah got up from the chair as he watched the young infiltrators drag two more young kids into the hospital in hopes of filling the infiltrators' hunger for destruction. Sanah knew that the infiltrators didn't need to kill or eat to survive; they could live forever without either of those. They killed for pure pleasure. "We need to make sure they accept the mass."

"They will," Salamor said, hovering over Sanah.

"She can still disrupt the plan," Sanah said. "We need her distracted."

"As long as her stability in the family is faltering we cannot lose," Salamor said.

***

Alex and Anne sat around the pizza table, laughing at Mole singing karaoke in honor of Anne. His singing was absolutely horrible, but he had the place cheering him on over his confidence and the embarrassment Anne was portraying.

"You go, babe!" Anne screamed as she laughed.

Alex was smiling as she sat and watched him. She thought she would never forgive herself for what she did to her family. Anne turned to Alex, smiling at her and patted Alex's hand on the table, telling her that everything was going to be alright. Even Komptin was wagging his tail with happiness between the three of them. Mole finished his song with a bow and the place erupted. "He really doesn't care, does he?"

"Not about embarrassing himself," Anne pointed out. "But when he loves, it is all in."

Mole came off the stage and came over to Anne. "I have to pee."

"Thanks for the update," Alex said.

Mole kissed Anne and he went off to the bathroom. Anne watched him leave and turned to take a bite of her vegetarian pizza.

"So, Anne, I heard you were in the finals for a paid Vatican study," Alex mentioned, chugging down her Apollo drink.

"Your source isn't quite up to date," Anne said, taking a sip of wine.

"Oh?" Alex said.

"Yeah, I got chosen," Anne said, swallowing her pizza.

Alex was happy for Anne, but she was worried about Mole and Anne, "Are you going to go?"

Anne shook her head yes, "I leave in two days."

"What about Mole?"

"Well, long story short, we are going to stay together. It's only six months and we are remaining with each other," Anne told her. "There's not a doubt in my mind we will be okay." Anne smiled at her. "And now that we—as in all of us—are back together, I have no worries."

Alex smiled back as she was kind of playing with her Apollo Energy can. "Anne, I need to apologize specifically to you."

Anne put her pizza down and turned to Alex, "It's okay, I und—"

Alex interrupted, "Anne please, I need to say this."

Anne shook her head as if to say, "Go ahead."

"I have strength, power, and can do stuff that would make the average comic book nerd turn green with envy," Alex told her, laying the foundation of her apology.

"Yes, yes you do," Anne confirmed.

"But let me tell you something. Your heart gives you more strength than I can ever have. You truly are an amazing person and I wish I could be half the person you are," Alex told her. "I am truly, truly, sorry for what I put you through, both physically," Alex slightly rubbed her neck in remembrance of Gastrix grabbing Anne's neck, "and emotionally."

"Alex," Anne said. "Don't worry about it. And let me tell you something: you and Kale are the two most important people in my life. I love you two so much and I'm going to miss you so much when I'm gone." Anne wiped her tears. "Promise me this, promise me that you take care of Kale while I'm gone."

"You know I will," Alex got up from the table with Anne and the two hugged and cried in each other's arms.

"Don't cry," Mole said, putting his arms around the both of them, coming back from the bathroom. "I'm right here."

"You're such an idiot, Mole," Alex said to him.

"I love you too," he said, putting his head on the two girls. "So, if you want us to give Gastrix another chance…"

"No, I'm going to end it tonight," Alex said. "I can't believe I allowed him to influence me like that. I thought I was stronger than that. It gave me a small taste of what Sara must have went through all those years."

"Don't beat yourself up," Mole told her. "Lord knows I've screwed some things up in my life but look at the end result. I have a beautiful girl who has chosen me to be her boyfriend," he said, grabbing her hand. "I have my best friend back, and most of all, I have humility."

"Humility?" Alex asked.

"A reminder that I have a disease and that I need to check myself every now and then," Mole said. "I need to attend at least two meetings a month to maintain my sobriety." The waitress came over with the bill. She handed it over to Mole. Mole grabbed and then tossed it at Alex. "You're paying," he smiled.

After Alex paid the bill, she joined Mole and Anne standing outside, looking up in the sky.

"What are you looking at?"

"The stars," Anne said. "They are really clear tonight."

Alex looked up and saw the Osiah star. She smiled at it and gave it thumbs up. "They truly are something special." She looked down at her watch, "Well, Gastrix should be getting up soon to go out. I guess I should get this over with."

"Do you want us to come with you?" Anne asked her, about to put on her coat.

"I got this," Alex winked at her. "Come on, Komptin."

Alex walked through the park where the street fair was up and running. The sounds of kids mixed with the smell of food filled the air. She enjoyed the atmosphere as she saw Celestial in the distance laughing with some young children playing fair games. Alex walked up to the nearest food vendor and ordered.

Celestial saw her coming. "Go on, children, have fun." Celestial gave one of the little girls a stuffed animal. "So innocent." She looked up at Alex. "And how are you?"

"I just wanted to come over to apologize," Alex said. "I'm the reason you were injured. My selfishness and pride almost got you killed.'

"Not the first time my Lite was almost extinguished," Celestial said. "Will not be the last."

"But still, I just want to say, I'm sorry," Alex said. "I'm actually on my way to break up with Gastrix."

"Be careful, Alexandria," Celestial said. "Some people just like to be angry."

"I will be fine," Alex leaned into hug Celestial.

Celestial hugged Alex, "I know you will." Celestial motioned to Ariel and Devine, "It is time to go."

Ariel and Devine nodded in agreement.

"Wait," Alex said. She looked to Ariel and Devine and handed them the greasy bag. "This is just a thank you."

Ariel and Devine grabbed the bag and opened it, "What is it?" they both asked.

"Deep fried Oreos," Alex said. The two of them picked them up and tasted them. Their faces lit up with excitement. They both smiled at Alex. She quietly whispered, "I really mean it, thanks."

The two guardians smiled and put their hands on Alex's shoulder before joining Celestial in the crowd.

***

Alex arrived at the small studio apartment where Gastrix was no doubt still lying in bed, waiting for her to come home. She sighed and opened the door. She saw him actually up and getting dressed which was a shock to her. She sat there studying him for a second, thinking to herself that he really wasn't what she wanted in a boyfriend.

"Where were you?" Gastrix asked.

"Getting some pizza," Alex told him, looking at how dirty the place was. There was an actual aroma in the air that was foul.

He got irritated with her answer, "How many times do I have to tell you that you're going to get fat eating like that," Gastrix glanced back at Alex's hands. "Don't you think I would have wanted something to eat?"

Alex shut the door behind her. Komptin walked towards an empty spot in the room where he stood in an over-watch position. "Gastrix, can we talk?"

"On the way to the club," he said. "Come on, let's go!"

"No, I wanna talk now," Alex said, not budging.

"Stop back-talking me. I don't want to talk, I wanna go out. Apparently, I need to stop and get something to eat before we go out," he snapped. He headed towards the door but then turned to look at Alex who wasn't moving.

"Gastrix, I think we both want something different out of life," Alex said. "I really think it would be better for the both of us to go our separate ways."

"Wait, are you trying to break up with me?" Gastrix came up to her, staring down, trying to intimidate her.

"Well, yah," Alex stared him in the eye. "Gastrix, I'm not happy with you."

"You little whore," Gastrix pointed a finger at her.

"Excuse me?" Alex said, standing up to him.

"You think you could toy with me. Do you think anyone would love such a little goth skank like you?"

"You're an ass," Alex said as she started to leave.

"You are not happy with me?" Gastrix asked her. "You don't know what happy is, let me show you." He grabbed her and threw her on the bed. "I will make you love me," He pinned her down and forced himself onto her. Alex heard Komptin start to walk over to her, she put up her finger, telling him to stand down. "You are such an ugly whore, you will get no one like me, ever."

"Well thank God for small favors," Alex told him.

Gastrix's face turned red with anger as he punched her in the face twice. "Don't you ever talk to me like that."

"Big mistake," Alex got her hands on his chest as she pushed him off with relative ease. She stood up, trying to control her temper. She could feel herself starting to pulsate.

Gastrix got up from the floor. He was so blind with rage he didn't realize that little Alex just threw him off of her like a rag doll. "No one, I mean no one, will ever love you."

Alex rolled her eyes and headed to the door. "You have till the end of the month to get out," Alex said "I'm outta here."

Gastrix was getting more furious. "You flat breasted hag." He started walking towards the door and he looked at Komptin. Komptin barked at him.

"Let's go, Komptin." The massive dog turned to leave with Alex when Gastrix kicked him full force, sending him into the wall.

"Stupid ass dog," Gastrix yelled at him.

Alex ran over to Komptin, petting him on his head. "You ok? Of course, you are," she said. Komptin looked over at Gastrix who was getting more upset.

"GET OUT, YOU BITCH!" Gastrix yelled.

Komptin looked back up at Alex. "Okay," Komptin's eyes flashed blue. Alex stood up and leaned against the wall. "Just for the record, I'm just here for protection."

"Oh, you going to protect your little doggy?" Gastrix asked.

Alex shook her head no, "I'm here to protect you."

Komptin growled and then morphed into his fighting state. Gastrix's eyes grew big as he screamed in a high pitch as he backed up against the wall. Komptin walked up to him, growling and snapping his massive jaw with drool coming from his mouth. Komptin put his massive head close to Gastrix's face as he stared at him.

Komptin drew closer and closer and then stopped and took a sniff. He looked down at Gastrix's pants and then looked back at Gastrix who was trembling with fear. "Oh, man," Alex said, waving her hands across her face. "Tell me you didn't." Komptin turned around, leaving Gastrix up against the wall in his soiled pants. "There goes my security deposit," Alex said, leaving the apartment. "Disgusting."

***

Welltore and Velcrown dragged the two young college kids through the abandoned hospital. The sound of the muffled screaming slightly echoed throughout the hallways. They tried grabbing anything they could, trying to get away. It seemed as if the girl was fighting harder than the guy they had captured from behind the bar. The two of them were scraping and clawing the floors, trying to escape. Their mouths were duct taped shut so the screams didn't carry far.

Velcrown picked up the young blonde girl and hung her from the ceiling. The boy was tied to the chair as the two of them were forced to look at each other. Sanah came into the room with Salamor floating behind. "Why did you bring them here?"

Sanah asked, looking at them. He grabbed the girl's chin and studied the fear in her eyes.

Welltore was the first to speak, "She smells like a Lite Sentry, so we thought she must be her."

"The Lite Sentry is small, petite, feisty…she is not the Sentry. There is no way she would have let you take her in this manner," Sanah said, slapping the blonde girl across the face. "Plus, the Lite Sentry will have a massive dog-like creature with her at all times." The blonde girl's eyes grew big. Sanah knew he said something that sparked in her mind, "Something you want to say?" The girl shook her head no. "Okay."

Sanah motioned to the infiltrators, releasing their anxiety for the kill. They seemed to sniff the boy's body before the first one bit off a chunk of arm. The boy tried to scream in pain but was muffled from the duct tape. The other infiltrators followed suit, slowly nibbling. The boy looked into Brenda's eyes before they vanished into darkness. The boy's body went limp as the rest of the infiltrators tore him apart like a pack of wild wolves fighting over a carcass.

Sanah ripped the duct tape off the girl's lips as she screamed and started crying. "I'm only going to ask you this once, why do you smell like the Lite Sentry?"

"I don't know what that is," the girl cried.

"She may have been tapped?" Sanah turned to Salamor.

"Tapped for what?" the girl pleaded.

Sanah wiped his face in agitation. He grabbed the girl by the hair and ears to yell, "Why do you smell like the Lite Sentry Alex!"

"I'm sorry, I borrowed her shirt, I didn't have time to give it to her before she moved out," the girl explained.

Sanah stepped back. "You know Alex," he motioned with his hand the height of Alex.

"Yes," she cried, "She's my roommate or used to be before she moved out."

"Why did she move out?" Salamor asked.

"Her and Anne along with Kale were fighting over something. Please, let me go," she pleaded.

Sanah looked over to the window, "I want the Sentry dead. She is without her support. She is alone and falling in faith. Now is the time for her demise. She will not stop the mass Infiltration."

Chapter 11

Alex was walking home after leaving the soiled-pants ex-boyfriend of hers. She had a sense of relief off her shoulders that night. She actually seemed happy. The sky was a little bit more clear than usual. She looked up the bright purple star shining above her. Alex was still deeply troubled because she knew she was going to have to go against Sanah. She had a gut feeling that it was going to be soon. She came across the church where she saw the Cardinal walk out with Father Tom. "Cardinal," Alex greeted him.

"Alexandria," the Cardinal smiled at her as Father Tom walked on. "How are you this evening?"

"I'm okay," she said, petting her dog. "What are you doing here?"

The Cardinal raised his eyebrows and gave a one chuckle laugh, "Actually, I just got out of a meeting with the Catholic Council in the Vatican about you."

Alex's gut started to turn, "Am I in trouble?"

He sat down on the steps of the church. "You are fine, we were discussing your role here and the role of your friend."

"Anne?" Alex asked. "Is she still going?"

The Cardinal nodded. "We just are trying to figure out what we are going to do with her upon her return. She's the first 'outsider' to see an infiltrator and live, not to mention the morphing of your little friend there."

"I handled it fine," Alex was scratching Komptin's head that was lying on her lap.

"You're also a Lite Sentry," Cardinal said. "Forgive me for this, she's, for lack of a better term, fully human."

Alex normally would have taken offense by that, but she knew she wasn't fully human. "What about the Catholic Council, they are made up of humans."

"We are also all a special division of the priesthood. Only a select few are brought in the councils," he looked over at the young priest. "We also have signed a permanent non-disclosure agreement if we indulge to the public."

Alex glanced side to side. "What if someone might have scared someone by way of their dog?"

The Cardinal put up his hands, "I don't want to know about it," he laughed, full well-knowing what she was insinuating. Alex joined him in sitting on the steps of the church overlooking the office next door. She stared at the office reconstruction from across the street. "Your doing?"

Alex verified his perception. "Ariel and Devine had a little talk with me."

"Ah," the Cardinal said. "And I'm assuming they got their message across."

"Yep," Alex said, rubbing the back of her head.

"Cardinal," the young priest came up to them. "I will call for the car."

"Thank you, father," the Cardinal said. The young priest walked down to the street level and got on the radio to speak to whom Alex was assuming was the Cardinal's bodyguard. "What's on your mind, child?"

"I'm good," Alex said. "When do you head back to D.C.?

"Three days," Cardinal Thomas said. "I'm a guest speaker at your college tomorrow night for the freshman class."

"Father Carl doesn't like me."

"No, no he doesn't," the Cardinal admitted. "I wouldn't worry about it."

"I'm not, but I think Father Tom doesn't like me either." She watched him with the Cardinal's bodyguard.

The Cardinal studied Alex's reaction towards him, "Why does that bother you?"

"Father Carl has no idea what I do, so for that ignorance, I can see why he doesn't like me. Father Tom knows what I do," Alex picked some dirt out of Komptin's fur.

"The only one you have to prove yourself to is yourself and God. Everyone else, doesn't matter," he told her.

She smiled at him.

"Please tell me, what's on your mind."

"For the first time in years, I'm scared," Alex said. "I know I could die at every hunt, but this one? This one is different."

"Why is that?"

"He's powerful, very powerful," Alex pointed out.

"Yes, but you have something more powerful that will get you through this."

Alex looked up at him, "Yah, what's that?"

"A heart full of faith," the Cardinal said. "Sanah had lost his faith and the Dark consumed him because he let it." He thumped her on her

220

chest. "Keep this, no matter what, and you'll be fine."

The car pulled up and the young priest opened the door, motioning to the Cardinal that his ride was ready.

"Cardinal," Alex said. "I just want to say, thank you for everything."

"Not a problem, dear," the Cardinal kissed her on top of the head. "Keep true to your faith." The Cardinal walked down to the steps of the car where the young priest was holding the door. He turned to wave to Alex, "You'll be fine."

Alex gave him a weary wave back. "I guess we need to find out what Sanah is up to."

***

Sanah summoned Velcrown and Welltore. "I need you to gather a meeting for tomorrow night at the old hospital on the other side of town."

Velcrown acknowledged the request. "How many do you wish?"

Sanah answered, "All of them."

"You got it," Welltore said.

Sanah walked through the hospital that once held the sick and dying. The sin of man that caused such pain in this world. The human race deserves to suffer. He walked into a room that must have been the nursery. He remembered his child being born. It was the happiest that he'd ever been. The thought of making sure he grew up in a world without worry raced through his mind.

No one cared about the death of his wife and son. He came home one night to find a demon in his living room holding his wife while an infiltrator surrounded his son. The fear for his family consumed him but he had to remain true to his faith. The demon had asked Sanah to willingly accept the infiltrator to inhabit him. If Sanah had allowed it, then the demon would have let one of his family members go. The demon would not let Sanah choose which family member would live. His wife screamed at Sanah not to accept the infiltrator, that they would meet him in Heaven when the time came. Sanah knew a person couldn't be infiltrated based on a threat, and so did the red-haired demon. He was just doing this out of pure enjoyment. He wanted him to choose.

Sanah prayed to give him strength as he watched the demon kill his wife and the infiltrator to tear apart his boy in front of him. He attacked the infiltrator, eventually killing it later that night. The demon that killed his wife was never seen again, but he would never forget him. His red hair that matched his glowing red eyes. He had never seen a demon that was able to produce a glowing red fist, but he had as it went through the body of his wife.

He had lost so much in this war and sacrificed so much. No one appreciated his fight in this war. The next generation of Sentry was beyond undisciplined. She was a representation of what this human race has become; an unfaithful, self-centered, narcissistic burden on this planet. The Dark, The Dark will put them in their place, make them pay for their sin. The sacrifice of Sanah's soul was a small price to ensure humanity fell to the power of the Dark.

***

Alex didn't want to feel like a third wheel in the car, so she decided to take a cab to the airport to see Anne off. She would drive Anne's car back with Mole to drop him off at the apartment. They decided that Alex and Mole would just stay in the apartment with Brenda; whom they hadn't seen for quite a while.

She met Mole and Anne who were outside the airport terminal, looking at each other. She could see Mole was fighting back the tears, but Anne was in full Niagara Falls. It kind of choked up Alex a bit, watching the two of them. Alex felt as if now was a good time to approach them. "Hey guys."

Anne wiped away some of her tears, "Hey." She knelt to give Komptin a good-bye hug and he returned it with rubbing the top of his head on her cheek. "Oh, I'm going to miss you." she said, scuffling up his head. Anne got up and gave Alex a hug. "Take care of him."

"I will," Alex said.

"And be careful," Anne added. 'I'm going to miss you."

"Don't worry about me," Alex said to her, giving Anne a false confidence that she wasn't worried.

The two pulled away from each other. They gave each other a quick, forced smile.

"Ms. McClure," a voice said to them.

"Yes?" Anne turned around to see who was calling her name.

"I'm Antonio Caesar," the man in the suit said. "I will be your escort to the Vatican. I understand that you speak Italian?"

Anne extended her hand, "Parlo abbastanza per cavarmela. Per favore chiamami Anne."

"Molto bene, e un piacere conoscerti," Antonio answered her. He looked over at Alex. "And this must be Ms. Alexandria Johnson."

Alex stepped back, concerned that he knew who she was, but then it clicked that he must work directly for the Council. "It is nice to meet you."

"It is an honor, Ms. Johnson," he shook her hand. He sat there and stared at her as if she were a celebrity.

"How do you know Alex?" Kale asked him.

"Ms. Johnson was Ms. McClure's…" he tried formulating the words. He looked to Anne, "Riferimento al personaggio?"

Anne smiled, "Character reference," she told Kale. Anne was hoping Kale bought it because she didn't have a character reference on her application. Anne knew that he was just covering his tracks by announcing he knew who Alex was.

"This is my boyfriend, Kale," Anne introduced him to her.

Kale shook his hand, "Nice to meet you, Mr. Caesar." Kale looked to Anne, "Do me a favor, will you please?"

"Si," Antonio caught himself staring at Alex.

"Take care of Anne, please. I will forever be in your debt," Kale asked.

"Of course, I will," Antonio said. "Are these your bags?"

She nodded. "What flight are we on? I never got any tickets."

"We have a private jet that will take us there, with a 3-day layover in England. There we will get some last minute items before you start your studies," Antonio told her.

"Private jet, fancy," Mole told her. "That's one hell of a scholarship program."

Alex could see she was getting nervous as Anne asked, "How many are in the study program?"

"Just you," Antonio answered. "Only a one student program. I will have all the answers for you along the way, but we do have to get moving."

Anne understood. "Well, I guess this is it," She took in a deep breath. Anne gave another hug to Alex and she turned to Kale. "Kale." The two of them looked at each other.

"I love you," the both of them said at the same time. They embraced each other in a passionate good-bye kiss. The two continued to hug, refusing to let each other go.

"Ms. McClure," Antonio was looking at his watch and then at the two of them. "Take your time."

The two parted. "I have something for you," Mole reached into his pocket and gave her a box. He looked to Antonio, "Here is the customs form, please don't let her see it."

Antonio grabbed the paper. Alex could see he was trying not to smile, "Of course."

"Promise me you will not open it until the date on the package. Promise me."

"I promise," Anne inspected the box. "I love you."

"Love you too," Mole said. They gave each other one last kiss before Anne walked away with Antonio. She turned around one last time, giving all three of them a final wave.

They all returned the wave as Komptin gave a loud bark. "What is so special about the date that she can't open that box until then?" Alex asked Mole who couldn't take his eyes off Anne until she disappeared past security.

"It was the day that I completed my Iron Man," Mole answered her while taking a drink of water.

"What's in the box?" Alex asked him.

"The flower she gave me when I crossed the finish line. I had it bronzed that week," he finally turned towards the parking lot.

"Oh, that's sweet," Alex said, rubbing his back. "I can't believe you kept it this long."

"Yah, I just hope the engagement ring attached to the flower is the right fit," he said, walking to the car.

Alex's eyes grew big, "Kale Moler!"

***

Alex decided to go for a hunt that night. She was tired of wondering, she got tired of being scared. She was going to find out what Sanah was up to. She actually had to go out and get a new outfit for the hunt as all her clothes were at the studio apartment. Alex was pretty sure that Gastrix had tossed all of her stuff into the garbage. She had cleared it through Father Tom to buy some clothes for her hunt. All he told her was, "Don't go overboard." Alex knew she didn't have to ask

226

permission, but she felt like she needed to prove to the Cardinal that she could be responsible.

She had bought a black leather vest to go over her dark blue long sleeve shirt. She bought a pair of black pants that seemed to fit just right. They were stretchy enough to kick but had a tough material to them. She ran her finger over her scar on her neck before putting on her collar. She sat there looking at her neon red hair. "I hate red," she told Komptin who was staring at her on the bed. She ran her fingers through her hair. "I need to go do something first."

***

Alex returned to the apartment after visiting the hair salon in her new woven hair. It was very similar to her hair prior to her wonderful boyfriend. She had asked the salon girl to tie it into a ponytail tight because she was going out to find Sanah. It was too bad that her first official boyfriend was the jackass he turned out to be. She knew that if she didn't have the power of the Lite, Gastrix would have probably really hurt her emotionally and physically.

She walked into the bedroom to apply her dark makeup. She looked in the mirror and she was Alex again, and she liked it. She looked to Komptin who was eagerly waiting by her bedroom door. "I guess you are ready to go." Alex opened the door and saw Mole with a suitcase in the living room. "Where are you going?"

"I'm going to go home for a bit," he said, looking at his phone.

"Is everything all right?" Alex opened an Apollo. This sweet taste of nectar had never tasted so good to her.

"Yeah, I'm good. It's just I didn't ask Anne's parents' permission to ask her to marry me...I hope I didn't put the cart before the horse."

Alex walked up to Mole and gave him a big hug and a kiss on the cheek. "I'm pretty sure they would be honored to have you as an addition to their family." Alex smiled at her brother, "Plus, technically, they get me as well." She playfully smiled at him. "How are you getting home?"

"I have to be at the airport in a couple of hours," Kale checked the time on his watch. "Do you have time to get a drink?"

"Just as long as you just have Coke," she winked at him.

"That much is for certain," he put his phone down on the end table. "I have to take a poo-poo, I'll be right back."

"You know, Mole, you don't have to tell me everything," Alex said. She sat down on the couch. Her mind went back to thinking how lucky she will be to have her best friend marry her brother. The two were just so perfect for each other. Who knew, that night at the lake, the simple gesture of Mole giving Anne a sweatshirt would lead into marriage? Alex was a bit envious of them. They actually found their soulmates. Mole's phone rang on the end-table.

"Can you grab that? It might be Anne calling," Mole yelled from the bathroom.

"Yah," Alex grabbed the phone. "Hello."

"Hello, Anne?" the voice said on the other end of the phone.

"No, this is Alex, Mole's sister."

"Oh hello, this is Kameron. Mole's old roommate. How are you? I don't think we ever officially met," he said.

"No, we haven't. Mole is in the restroom, I will say you called," Alex said to him as she picked up the remote to the television. The cracked screen of the TV was staring back at her. She got embarrassed as she knew what that television represented.

"That would be great, thank you very much. I hope you have a nice evening," he said.

"Yep, you too," Alex said, hanging up the phone.

Mole came out of the bathroom, "Who was it?"

"Your old dorm roommate," Alex said. "Ready?"

"Yep."

***

Alex went to the park after dropping Mole off at the airport. It was a typical Friday night in the park. The food vendors were out trying to sell their products to a bunch of young adults who didn't know any better. Speaking of which, Alex was really in the mood for deep fried Oreos. She purchased the delight from a vendor and bought Komptin a hot dog. She sat down on a park bench overlooking the crowd. She was getting a bit nervous because she didn't feel any presence of an infiltrator or anything in the air that someone had

229

infiltrated. "Well, we are not going to find anything just sitting here on the park bench." Alex slapped her hands on her legs and sprung up and bumped into a kid running with a pamphlet in his hand. "Oh, I'm sorry," Alex said, helping him up.

"I'm going to be late," He got up and ran off.

"Must have a hot date or something," Alex told Komptin. She picked up the pamphlet the kid dropped, "Hey, you dropped..." She looked at the Freedom Off Religion pamphlet. She saw another girl holding the same pamphlet heading in that direction. "Excuse me."

The girl stopped, "I don't have time to talk, I gotta go." The girl just blew by Alex and took off.

"Must be some meeting," Alex said.

"Oh, look, the girlfriend of our 'good friend' Gastrix," a voice behind her said.

Alex turned around and saw two girls dressed in neon green with a cybergoth style to them. "Do I know you?"

"I'm Shelly, this is Tori," one of them said. "We've seen you at the clubs with Gastrix."

Alex was a bit embarrassed, "Well, if Gastrix is a friend of yours, you really need to re-evaluate your taste in friends."

"Oooo, someone is feisty...I like that," Tori said. "I take it you two broke up."

"You could say that," Alex said.

"Did he hurt you?" Shelly asked while examining her.

"He tried," Alex admitted.

Both Tori and Shelly looked at each other and then back at Alex, "And?"

"Well, let's just say he didn't really make it to the bathroom when he should have," Alex waved her hands in front of her nose, mocking a bad smell.

"I like her," Shelly said.

Alex watched another girl with one of those pamphlets walk by, heading in the direction where the others were. "Must be something going on with that organization."

"What organization is that?" Shelly asked, eating popcorn out of Tori's hand.

"The F.O.R.," Alex said.

"Those nutcases?" Tori said. "They have been all over the web advertising for a 'Freedom Off Religion' power meeting. Something about obtaining 'true' power."

Shelly chimed in, "Yah, it's a really weird location too. You had to RSVP to even be let in."

Alex looked in the direction the people were going, "Yah, where is it at?"

Tori looked at her phone, looking up the location, "Yeah, that's what I thought; it is at the old hospital."

Alex spat out her energy drink, "What?!"

"Is there a problem?" Shelly asked.

"Oh, damn it," Alex said. "You needed to RSVP to this thing? Does it say how many people are allowed to attend?"

"No, but do you want to get in?" Tori said. "I can get you in, no problem."

"Getting in is not the problem, it's going to be getting out," Alex said. She turned to them, "It doesn't say who's all going?"

"Oh, honey, are you wanting to know who's attending?" Tory asked with a sympathetic look.

"I just need a number of who's attending," Alex said.

Tori and Shelly sat down, "Ah, that will be easy."

"What are you doing?" Alex asked.

"Getting you your answer," Shelly said. Tori went into Shelly's backpack and pulled out a little portable computer. She started typing away.

Alex peeked over her shoulder to see a bunch of computer jargon on the screen. "This is way above my solitaire." Even Komptin tried to take a look at it.

"Don't forget to set the fourth algorithm or we are going to be groveling for the next hour," Shelly pointed to the screen.

"Yeah, I got it," Tori said. "38." She slammed her notebook down. "Time?"

"Five minutes, 49 seconds," Shelly said. "You're getting slow."

"Oh, you are going to pay for that," Tori grabbed Shelly's chin and kissed her.

"Promise?" Shelly asked.

"If you would excuse me, but I need to go," Alex said. "I owe you."

"Don't worry about it," the two of them said at the same time.

Chapter 12

Alex caught up with one of the people carrying a pamphlet. Alex was pretty sure they didn't know what was in store for them. If they accepted infiltration, then Alex would have to deal with a massive increase of Hosts. If they didn't accept infiltration, the Dark would kill them. Either or, Alex had to stop it. "Excuse me!" she yelled at a small boy. "Where are you going?" She knew full well where they were heading. The boy just ignored Alex and continued to head towards the hospital.

Alex walked on, hoping she wouldn't run into a demon. If she did, they would sense her Lite and then all hell would break loose. That would lead to a massacre and top of that, Alex knew she wouldn't survive the attack. She found a spot in the shadows in the alley, hiding from anyone who might see her so she could regain her game plan. "Komptin, I need to figure out what room they are meeting in." Alex ducked down from the sounds of people walking close by. "More than likely they are meeting in the cafeteria or one of the bigger rooms." Alex looked around her surroundings. "The only advantage is that they don't know we are coming. Hopefully, we can surprise them before infiltration begins." Alex looked to her companion who was on high alert. "Of course, surviving would be a bonus as well." She reached into her coat pocket and pulled out a can of Apollo. She cracked it open and took a drink. "You wanna know a scary thought. Can you imagine that there are that many willing people to be infiltrated?" Alex just shook her head at the disbelief that many people would give up their souls for a short-term promise of absolute power.

Komptin immediately morphed into his fighting state as he turned to the darkness of the alley behind him. He leaped into the dark at a pair of glowing red eyes staring at them. Alex instinctively ignited her Lite to join her fighting companion. Even though it was dark, the light from her fists provided enough light to see the snarling teeth and red eyes of the infiltrator.

Komptin was off to one side while Alex was on the other. The two circled the beast who was trying to decide if it was going to fight or try to make a break for it. In true infiltrator fashion, it didn't care about its own life as it charged Alex. Komptin grabbed its leg as Alex reversed from being prey to become the attacker. Her fist pulsated into the beast's face and body. The Infiltrator swung its head, knocking Alex into the side of the building. Komptin, still holding on to its leg, whipped the infiltrator into the side of the dumpster. The infiltrator went to regain its ground when Alex jumped into the air, punching it on top of the head. She grabbed its head and smashed into the side of the dumpster, causing a dent. She sensed the infiltrator was at a point of weakness. She formed a stabbing weapon and thrust it into the side of its neck. It howled in pain as it dissipated.

"Well, if we have over thirty-eight of those to go through, we are in for a long night," Alex stretched out her neck. "Are you up for this?"

Komptin turned to look at her, flashing his big blue eyes.

***

They headed in the direction of the hospital to try to disrupt the meeting before all the infiltration took place. She knew the infiltrators became more powerful once they inhabited a human. She peeked out and saw a person heading towards the hospital. He was a lot bigger than she was, but then again, almost everyone was. The kid walked by and Alex easily grabbed him and threw him to the ground. "Tell me where the meeting is taking place."

The kid, trembling in fear, said, "The hospital."

"No kidding," Alex flashed her eyes. "Where in the hospital?"

"Oh damn!" The kid got scared. "I don't know, I swear. They were going to tell us once we got there."

A frustrated Alex turned to Komptin. "I guess we are going to have to do this the hard way." She turned her attention back to the boy. "You see my big purple friend here. You know the gargoyle creature with glowing eyes."

The scared kid nodded yes.

"He's a puppy dog compared to what is waiting for you in that hospital. I suggest you go home and find something positive to do," She let him up. "Now get the hell out of here." She kicked him in the butt in the opposite direction of the hospital. "This is so gonna suck." She jumped up on the fire escape and climbed up to the top of the roof. Komptin jumped on the side of the building and climbed up to the roof by digging his claws into the brick. They both sat down, hiding from sight behind a shed on the roof. She sat there quietly for a bit before she spoke. "We are going to have to do this alone," she said. "It's too dangerous for Celestial to ask Ariel and Devine for assistance. I'd ask Sanah for help, but he's the one we are going after." She took a deep breath. "It's a weird feeling knowing you are going to die tonight." Komptin's sad face stared at Alex. She got up, "Let's get this over with."

* * *

Sanah looked over the crowd as they were coming in. It was a generally young crowd of people in their early to mid-twenties. His plan for a mass infiltration would tip the scale in this region. The infiltrators could walk among the humans and start putting an end to this destructive conflict.

One of the guests walked up to Sanah. He could feel himself getting annoyed by the mere fact he wanted to talk to him. "What?" Sanah asked.

"I was asked to let you know we now have thirty-seven people," the boy said.

"How many RSVP'd?" Sanah asked.

"Thirty-eight," the boy said.

"Okay," Sanah said. "You can leave now." He continued to scout out the window. He knew she was close. She was going to try to disrupt Sanah's plan. He wasn't too worried. If the shoe was on the other foot, he would have a hard time rescuing these people. He didn't think he would have the capability to pull it off. So, the fact that this Sentry was undisciplined, weak, young, and inexperienced didn't worry him.

"I just want to say, I speak for everyone that Jack and Cheri speak highly of your gift to us. Everyone in this room is eager for you to show it to us."

Sanah just shook his head and then shooed him away. He turned to the dark shadow hiding behind the light. "How many infiltrators did you get?"

"We have forty-five," Salamor answered him.

"Okay, leave thirty-seven, send the rest to guard the perimeter," Sanah commanded. "You should go too. If they spot anything, report back to me."

Salamor reluctantly hissed as he went into the shadows.

***

Sneaking into the complex wasn't going to be as difficult as she thought. They must have not infiltrated enough bodies to cover the perimeter. Really all she had to do was jump the fence, which she could do quite easily. The only problem was that she had no idea where she was going once she got into the hospital. There were plenty of rooms to hold forty people. With the mass infiltration that they were planning, the infiltrators would jump into them with ease. Alex just couldn't believe that forty plus people would allow themselves to get infiltrated.

She waited for a minute or two, observing the two individuals at the gate. "Looks like they are ready to go into the building," she said. "We should take one of those guards before they leave to find out where the meeting is." Alex got into a stance to attack. She was about to leap when she noticed movement on the roof. "Always something," she said, "Infiltrators are on look out on top of the hospital." She looked to Komptin who was looking behind him with a slow growl and flashing blue eyes. She turned around and saw the shadowed mist with red eyes. "Salamor!" Alex said.

"Lite Sentry!" he hissed. Komptin leaped at Salamor, passing through the body of Salamor, crashing his head into the brick wall behind him. He shook it off with an embarrassed growl. Even though his eyes were pure red with evil, Alex could have sworn she saw him roll his eyes. "Stupid creature." Salamor turned his attention to Alex. "Sanah will be very interested to see you here."

"Infiltration will not take place," Alex told him.

"There's nothing you can do to stop it," Salamor said. "Part of me would like to see Sanah destroy you, but I know you have a friend that is all alone...maybe I could end his pain." Even though Alex knew that Mole was safe and had gone back home to ask for permission to marry Anne, just the mere thought of the evilness in Salamor pushed her over the edge. "What? What are you going to do, pathetic mortal?" Alex lit her fists and pushed out a beam of light at Salamor, pushing him against the brick wall. He screamed in shock and pain as he started to lose his form. "How? This isn't possible."

"Die, you Dark, black-hearted Tinkerbell!" Alex pushed the light harder onto his body. Alex's determination to put an end to Salamor was interrupted as she was tackled by an infiltrator.

Alex and Komptin both turned their attention to the red-eyed black creature. Salamor dropped to the ground in pain and weak from the physical attack. The Dark Myst regained his composure and tried to fly before Alex caught him with her glowing hands. She grabbed his leg, preventing him from flying away, "If I see you again, I'm going to kill you." She forced a beam of Lite into the chest of Salamor, pushing him away in a scream of terror into the night. She turned her attention to the infiltrator who had his hands full with Komptin. Komptin already had it weakened, so Alex jumped on its back and jabbed a light knife into the back of the head. It howled in pain before disappearing into the ground. "Crap, I hope we weren't spotted and someone ran to Sanah." Alex looked to the main gate where two young kids were keeping guard. "I guess we should go through the front door."

***

Alex walked up to the two guarding the gate with their clipboards and nothing else. Alex knew the Dark was present; it overpowered her senses to see who was a Host or just a human. Alex had Komptin next to her in his dog-state hoping they would just let her go in.

"Who are you?" the girl asked her very abruptly.

"My friend told me to come to this meeting, said it would be a good time," Alex replied.

"And that?" the boy said, pointing to the dog.

"He's my diabetic canine. He lets me know when my blood sugar is down," Alex quickly replied.

"Do you know what this meeting is for?" the girl asked.

"As far as I know, it prevents religion from overtaking our lives," Alex said. She was hoping they were buying it.

"Go ahead," the girl said.

"Cool," Alex said, walking through the gate. "Come on, boy," Alex motioned to Komptin, who started following her through the gate. She looked down to her partner as if telling him it seemed as if they made it. Something caught Alex's eye as she was walking into the compound. There was a small group of infiltrators gathered on the rooftops of nearby buildings staring down at her. "Oh, crap." A female hand grabbed her shoulder with demon claws. Alex didn't hesitate. She grabbed the hand and twisted it, causing the demon inhabited body to flip onto the ground. The infiltrated girl hissed with her red eyes while she was lying on the ground. Alex ignited her fists and went to strike the girl but she got jumped by the boy.

Komptin was distracted by two infiltrators that appeared from the darkness of the shadows. They attacked Komptin at full force as he morphed into his gargoyle state. They managed to knock him into a pile of metal barrels, having them pile onto his massive body.

***

Sanah heard a loud noise from outside the window. He made sure not to cause any suspicion as he walked over to the window to see what was going on. He knew that Alex had come to stop this Infiltration. He looked around the room to make sure that no one was paying attention to what was going on outside.

He looked to the leader of the group and told him to start the process. He went around and shut the blinds to make sure no one saw Alex trying to fight through. Luckily, there were two infiltrated demons and a group of infiltrators to keep her busy. He knew she couldn't survive the fight of two demons attacking her.

***

It has been a while since Alex had faced someone who had been infiltrated. As she recalled it wasn't a pleasurable experience. "I suppose we can't talk about this?" She stood up, patting the dirt off herself. The two demons hissed at her while flashing their red eyes.

"Tonight, you are going to die, Lite Harlot," the girl screamed at her as she charged at Alex.

Komptin was too busy fighting the infiltrators to try to clear a way into the hospital. Alex knew she had to take care of this herself. The demon charged at Alex in response to the attack. Alex quickly stepped to the side, swiping the leg of the female demon, sending her flying into the windshield of a parked car. Alex didn't have time to relish her small victory as the male demon threw the clipboard at Alex, hitting her on the nose,

241

causing it to bleed. "Really? A clipboard?" She looked at the blood dripping from her nose.

The male demon shrugged his shoulders. "It's all I had," he innocently said as he started to circle around.

Alex matched his circle, both wondering when the other was going to pounce. "You can still walk away from this."

"Can you?" he asked her.

"You know I can't," Alex said to him.

"I've always wanted to taste Lite Sentry," he licked his lips.

"Why are you all so disgusting?" she asked.

"I don't expect you to understand, I just expect you to do one thing," the male demon admitted to her.

"Yah, what's that?" Alex said.

"Forget about the other one."

Alex turned to see a demon claw swipe at her head, cutting the side of her face with one of her claws. Alex screamed in pain as she spun around to get away from her two attackers. She was back against the fence as the two approached. The blood dripping from her face was all that distracted Alex from the searing pain. Alex put her hand on the side of her face, trying to stop the blood. The two approached her and she charged at them. She dropped to the ground, tumbling in a summersault and quickly getting up. She didn't hesitate as she continued to run towards the hospital.

***

Sanah watched the group start to settle in their chairs. He was wondering why he had not heard from Salamor. The group was getting uneasy at being locked in the room. The room was a lecture hall where the group was all standing. There was a small platform where Warcourt was overlooking, watching the group.

"Please, we are about to get started," Warcourt announced. "Settle down." He motioned with his hands for everyone to be quiet.

"We were told that this was an F.O.R. meeting," one of the people said.

"I promise, all will be revealed to you soon," Warcourt said to the group. "But first, there is something I must ask you, and I really need a genuine answer."

***

Alex managed to escape the two demons to the backside of the hospital. Even though it was rare that she ran out of breath, she was breathing heavier than usual. She tried a door, but it was locked. She looked around for anything she could use to break the lock open. Komptin would normally barge through the door but he was clearing the infiltrators from the rooftop. She didn't like being separated from Komptin when she was in a battle. She didn't like the feeling of being alone.

There was a parked car in the parking lot. She looked around before running over to it. She ducked behind the car, snuck around to the window and tried opening the backdoor to the car. To her surprise it actually opened. "Thank God for small favors," she said beneath her breath. She crawled up to the front of the car and popped the trunk. She made it to the trunk and grabbed the tire iron and got to the one of the windows of the first floor. She could ignite her fists and break the glass but she was trying to stay as stealthy as possible. She did another look around and swung the tire iron, smashing the window. She crawled through the window and landed on the floor.

She got up, slowly opened the door to the office and peered out into the hallway. To her luck the bathroom was right across the hall. She ran across and made it into the bathroom. She couldn't see in the dark. She lit one of her fingers for some light and did a quick reconnaissance to see if she was alone before walking up to the mirror. There were still paper towels in an old dispenser. She grabbed a couple to wipe her face. The cut was deep and reached from her eye all the way down to the side of her face. She shivered from a chill going down her spine.

She extinguished her Lite when she heard the faint sound of two people talking from down the hallway. Alex silently made it to the door and stayed hidden in the darkness. She could hear the people talk but they did not sound like demons. She put the tire iron down because she did not want to kill any humans. Their ignorance didn't warrant a death sentence. The two of them walked by the doorway to the bathroom and Alex allowed them to pass before she came up behind them to cover their mouths, dragging them into the room where she had broken into. Alex uncovered their mouths while putting her finger to her lips. "Shhhhh."

"Who are you?" one of the boys asked her.

"Dude, this is the one that we were told to look out for!" the other boy said, trying to get up, but Alex grabbed him by the jacket. She threw him against the wall like a rag doll. She picked up the other boy, turned him around and kicked him towards the one she had thrown, knocking them into each other.

"Sit," she commanded. She looked around to ensure she wasn't going to get attacked again from behind. "Where's the meeting?" The two boys just looked at each other and then didn't say a word. "Is this how we are going to play this?" Alex lit her fists and punched the wall next to one of the boys' heads, going through the wall.

"Fourth floor lecture hall," both boys said immediately.

"You will die before you make it up there, though," one of the boys laughed.

"Do you even know what is about to happen tonight?" Alex asked them.

"Yeah, we are going to make this country free of all religion through absolute power," the other said.

Alex just rolled her eyes. She picked one of them and put him in a headlock while her foot was on the other one's throat, preventing him from screaming. The boy she had in a headlock passed out and she gently put him on the floor. "You're a crazy bi…"

Alex lifted up her finger, "Don't say it, I'm saving your life." She grabbed him, knocked him out, putting them next to each other, and tucked away in the corner. She ripped a drape off the windows and covered the boys up. She hoped that no one would find them.

She stepped out into the hallway and found the first set of stairs. She made sure she was alone. She made it to the first landing when she heard the door open to the stairwell below her. She took a couple of steps up the stairwell to peek down at who was coming. It was the two demons she was fighting earlier. She knew she was in trouble. She was in a confined space and she had to prevent them from reaching Sanah to let him know where she was. She had no choice; she was going to have to fight them. Here and now. She took a deep breath and leaped down, throwing a Lite Beam down on the girl while she fell on top of the male demon.

The male demon stood up with Alex on his chest and threw her into the wall. An imprint of Alex's body was left as the demon picked her up and head butted her in the mouth. More blood poured from Alex's lip as she was dazed and could feel her body going limp.

"Go tell Sanah we have the Lite Sentry," he told the female. Her eyes flashed red and was on her way up the stairs when Alex shot another beam of light straight into the eyes of the male demon. He screamed in pain, holding his eyes, banging his head against the wall in a fit of rage. Alex dropped to the ground and then instantly leaped towards the stairs to grab the female demon's ankle. With all her might, she pulled the demon to the floor. The demon flipped herself around and started to kick Alex in the face multiple times. Alex, in a fit of rage yanked down on the leg of the demon, causing her to slide down the stairs. She continued to punch the demon in the face ferociously. The demon forcefully grabbed Alex's thigh and dug her claws into her leg. Alex could feel the demon claws dig deeper and deeper. She grabbed the demon's hair and lifted her head to smash it against the corner of the stairs. It howled in pain just as Alex speared it through her eye before the body dissipated into the air.

Alex turned to the male demon who just recovered from the Lite Beam in his eyes. His eyes were scarred and full of hate as he pushed Alex back into the wall. He continued to punch Alex in her side. She felt a rib crack just before she had an opportunity to break free from the attack. She jumped over the banister. When she landed, she felt a bit weak as she started to spit out blood. The male demon came up behind her and pushed her face first into the wall as it punched her in the back. She just dropped to the ground in between punches, causing the demon to smash its hand against the wall. Alex managed to get to her feet, facing it. Bloody, torn, and feeling weak, Alex took what energy she had left for a full charge. The male demon was shocked at the attack where he didn't have time to counter. Alex jumped in the air and managed to land a punch on top of the bridge of the demon's nose. She turned him around to face the wall and bashed his face into it. She punched the demon in the sides as he howled in pain. He elbowed Alex in her open wound. She stopped her attack and turned around to hold her face. The demon took advantage of this moment of weakness and managed to claw on her back, Alex dropping to her hands and knees. She spat out more blood as the demon kicked her in her side. It sent her flying back into the wall. He went to kick her again, but she grabbed his leg. With her lit fist she punched him in the crotch, sending him to the ground. Alex formed a knife and stabbed him in the throat, causing the demon to disappear.

Alex dropped to the ground, holding her side. She felt ashamed as she started to uncontrollably cry from the pain. She wiped her tears and spat out a mixture of snot and blood. She managed to push herself up on all fours before being able to stand up. She felt regret as she saw how many stairs she was going to have to climb. After swallowing hard, Alex limped up the stairs to the third floor. She hadn't heard any sign of Komptin, now in fear that he was outmatched by the infiltrators on the roof. She looked at the directory to the third floor and saw that she was just a couple of doors down from the hospital chapel. She slowly opened the door to see if any infiltrators or demons were present. She managed to limp into the chapel to sit down in the first pew. She wanted to test her theory in hopes that it worked. She tried to ignite her fists, but it did not work. She was in a sanctuary; a much-needed sense of security.

The pain she felt as she laid down for a couple of minutes was intense as she tried to prevent more tears from falling. She rested for a short time to try to regain her strength. She got up to look at the cross lying down on the altar. She limped up to it and placed it upright. She sat down, looking at it. "Hey there," she wiped another tear from her face. She looked at her finger at the tear, but it was mostly made of blood. She looked down at her wounds and felt the blood drip from her head. She didn't know what to say. She just looked up at the stained-glass window, using her last bit of strength not to cry. "Well, I hope I made You proud. Please just keep an extra eye on Mole and Anne for me." She just tried to smile and nodded up at Him. "Thanks." She went to get up and saw a figure in black sitting in the pews across from her two rows back. The pure hate of the representative of the Dark looked up from under his big black hat. His pale white face showed through its greasy black hair. The smell of rotting flesh filled the room. He just looked at Alex and smiled.

"Good evening," he said.

Alex just sighed and sat back down. A sudden burst of determination filled her with strength. She was not going to give him the satisfaction of watching her in pain. Out of disbelief that Vandor was there, Alex just said the first thing that came to her mind. "How ya doin?"

"I'm all right considering, thank you for asking," Vandor looked down at a pool of her blood on the ground. He touched it with his finger and licked it. "I really do love the taste of Lite Sentry."

Alex knew that the second she stepped out of the chapel, Vandor could attack, easily ending her life and mission. "Well, it looks like I'm not going anywhere soon," she told him. "I'm not going to give you the satisfaction."

Vandor smiled, "I can see why Osiah liked you."

"I can honestly say that seeing your ugly face is not really the last thing I want to see before I die, so if you will excuse me, I'm going to turn my attention to Him," Alex turned around to look at the cross.

"Has he ever truly answered you?" Vandor asked her out of curiosity.

Alex turned to him. "Yes," she answered as if it was the dumbest question she has ever heard.

Vandor was shocked, "Really?"

"Not directly, but I wouldn't expect you to understand with your limited brain capacity," Alex said back to him. "Now if you will excuse me." She rolled her eyes as she shook her head.

Vandor snickered. "Perceptions, but I can give you what you truly desire."

Alex continued to face forward, "It would be just an illusion of the truth."

"Isn't an eternal illusion better than knowing you will never have it?" Vandor got up and whispered in her ear. "All you have to do is say 'yes'."

She turned around to face him, "I hope He takes me soon, because I don't want to sit here for hours listening to you."

Vandor stood straight up to walk around in front of Alex and sat down, staring at her. "Look at me."

Alex at first refused but then she took a look at him without moving her head. "What?"

"Have I ever lied to you?"

Alex looked back at all her interactions with Vandor, "I can honestly say 'no' to that." She turned her attention back to the crucifix.

"Then hear me and listen," Vandor said. "I promise, and without asking anything in return, I promise you, that I will not hurt you when you leave this sanctuary."

Alex peered at him.

"I promise, I will not harm you when you leave," Vandor told him. "I'm giving you a gift and asking nothing in return."

"I can just walk out and you are not going to do anything or do you have one of your minions right outside the doorway?" Alex asked him in disbelief.

"I'll even tell you, nothing on this floor will hurt you within my control," Vandor promised her. Alex got up and limped towards the chapel exit. "Remember, little one, all you have to do is say 'yes'," he grinned.

Alex got to the exit and peered out, looking back and forth. She didn't hear or see anything. She turned around to look at Vandor and he just waved at her. She stepped out into the battlefield and lit her fists to make sure she didn't inadvertently agree to something she didn't mean to. Still blue. She sighed in relief as she walked up the stairs to the fourth floor.

***

Warcourt continued to speak. "For far too long this world has been in constant conflict over 'His' name!" he air-quoted. "The Muslims hate the Jews, the Lutherans hate the Catholics, the Catholics hate everyone. People hide behind 'His' name to justify genocide!" he screamed. "It's time for that to end by eliminating all religion from this country!"

The crowd cheered in acceptance. Sanah leaned on the back wall overlooking the crowd. He peered out the window and didn't see any sign of the Lite Sentry or his two guards at the gate. He still wondered why he hadn't heard from Salamor yet.

"How are we going to achieve this?" someone yelled from inside the crowd

"Through acceptance of the power I'm going to offer you!" Warcourt yelled. "Now I ask you, will you accept my offer?!" He motivated the crowd.

***

Alex heard the cheering from the middle of the hallway. She wasn't amazed but still was surprised that Vandor had kept his word. She had had no signs of demons or infiltrators since her little conversation. She walked down to the doorway of the lecture hall where people were cheering. Alex leaned against the wall of the entryway. She knew she would not be walking out of this room tonight.

***

Sanah turned his attention to the doorway of the lecture hall. "Alex," he growled.

Warcourt continued his speech, "Now my friends, absolute power can be frightening, but everything is frightening if you don't understand it. To understand it, you must accept it! Are you willing to accept it?"

The crowd cheered, "Yes! Yes!"

Warcourt smiled at Sanah who motioned to him to hurry-up. "My friends, behind this door is absolute power, now drop to your knees and accept this power!" Warcourt walked to the curtains, ready to open them. "True power is frightening. Don't be afraid, just accept with open arms!"

The crowd cheered.

Warcourt pulled back the curtains to a group of infiltrators. The crowd cheered as they all dropped to their knees with their arms open. The infiltrators growled as they were about to leap.

***

Alex got a sudden burst of energy and she burst open the door, shooting a Lite Beam at Warcourt. It knocked him down the podium into a group of infiltrators. The crowd screamed, running amuck trying to get away. The infiltrators howled at the anger of not being able to become demons.

"BITCH!" Sanah screamed as he shot a beam of his own at Alex. She dodged out of the way. Sanah's beam caught a member of the crowd, pushing him against the wall, crushing all the bones in his body. The body dropped lifeless. "Not one can make it out alive!" Sanah screamed. "Kill them, kill them all!"

The infiltrators attacked while some of the crowd made it to hallways and to exits to escape the carnage. Alex fended off some of the infiltrators, while, to her surprise, some of the humans were trying to stop her as well. She was trying to muscle her way through infiltrators to Sanah. Alex watched Sanah fighting his way to her, killing anybody that was getting in his way. A loud explosion came from the wall as Komptin broke through, looking at the situation. He was scratched with blue blood dripping from his open cuts. He gave a massive roar which startled most the people in the room.

"Komptin! Protect the people! Give them safe passage out of here!" Alex screamed.

Komptin attacked the infiltrators as they were trying to slaughter the people. A group of the infiltrators attacked the gargoyle, pushing him back to a corner as he tried to fend them off. Alex felt sorry she couldn't help her friend as she approached Sanah. "I'm sorry, Sanah" she told the former Lite Sentry with glowing purple eyes.

"You and these humans are all pathetic," Sanah told her. "You all will be diminished tonight." He grabbed her and they both struggled as they tried to wrestle each other. They fell out the window, landing on a rooftop a couple of floors down. Alex shook her head, trying to get the cobwebs out. She looked to see where Sanah was, half hoping he had something impaled through his chest.

She struggled to her feet where he, too, was getting up. "We don't have to do this. We can still save these people."

"I'm done saving people who don't appreciate life or care for others," Sanah said. "I've seen more death, more sins, more Dark in people than you will ever see!" Sanah looked down at the people trying to escape as they were grappled by infiltrators, ripping them to shreds.

Alex too was looking down, each death making her feel guilty for not being able to help them. She heard Komptin upstairs fighting through his share of infiltrators, trying to protect who he could. "Is this what your wife and child would want?" Alex pleaded with him.

Sanah looked down at the mass carnage. "It was how they ended up. You can't stop the Dark." He turned to Alex with his purple fists lit. "So, I joined with it to end this war!" Sanah stepped back to see Alex do the same. "When the time comes, you too, will lose all hope in the Lite." The two stared at each other before Sanah shot a Lite Beam at Alex and she in return did the same. It met in the middle, causing a bright shockwave that echoed throughout the sky. The pulse knocked both Sanah and Alex off the rooftop, landing on the ground. All the infiltrators were thrown off their feet, sending some of them into trees, lampposts, and cars. The humans that were trying to escape were tossed in the air and crashed to the ground. They somehow managed to regain consciousness before the infiltrators and ran out of the park.

Alex got up from of all fours and managed to stand up, looking at Sanah who, too, was trying to gain his bearing. "Okay, let's agree not to do that again," she joked, trying to retain her equilibrium.

"That is why you fail as a Sentry; you can't take anything serious!" He lit his fists for a full-frontal attack on Alex. She did not have time to properly defend herself. He easily managed to punch her straight to the ground, followed by a kick to her side. Alex felt Sanah grab her by the hair to lift her to her feet. He grabbed her in a headlock, putting his arms around her throat. "Don't fight it, just accept your fate! Let the darkness overtake you" He squeezed as hard as he could.

Alex dropped to the ground, driving Sanah's chin into the top of her head. It dazed Sanah enough to loosen his grip on her. She stepped to the side with Sanah still holding onto her neck. She mustered all her strength and grabbed his legs to lift him up. She fell backwards, bringing Sanah crashing to the ground. Alex saw that he was stunned and went on the offensive. "I don't want to kill you!" She grabbed him and threw him into the side of a semi-trailer sized dumpster. His body collided into the metal tub. She ran up to him and grabbed his shirt. She gave continuous punches to his face. He blocked one of the punches and twisted her arm, returning a massive hit across her cheek, causing her to stumble backwards.

"There is no way you are going to kill me. You lack conviction, you lack discipline," Sanah told her as he looked at his hand from wiping the blood from his face. "You are a worthless Sentry."

"Still made you bleed," she told him with her eyes glowing blue, then she ran at him. He swung at her as she ducked and slid behind him. Sanah jumped when Alex tried to swipe his legs. As he was landing, he punched her on the side of her face where her massive wound was. Alex's head was shot with pain as she dropped to the ground. She grabbed her face as the pulsating sense of pain rushed through her head.

"Oooo, that's a bad one," Sanah smiled as he analyzed his opponent. He caught his breath and walked up to her. He punched her again on the side of the face. Alex fell to the ground again. She slowly got to her hands and knees. He walked over to her and pushed her over with his foot as she laid on her stomach, trying to get up. Sanah picked her up from behind, putting his arms around her neck again. "Don't worry, I know that look. That is the look of defeat." He lit his finger into a sharp point and started cutting into the wound on the side of Alex's face. The feeling of Sanah's Lite was a pain like Alex had never felt before. The burning pain seemed to trickle through her whole body. "Ever wonder what happens to a Lite Sentry after death?" Sanah looked to the stars. "You're no angel, so no star...you're not a full human and you failed Him as a Sentry...so do you think He will let you into Heaven?" He let go of Alex and spun her around, again punching her on the side of face. She dropped to the ground, unable to move. "Do me a favor and let me know." Sanah formed a spear and was about to thrust it into Alex when Komptin came and jumped at Sanah. He immediately thrust the spear into Komptin's chest. Blue blood spattered as Komptin howled in pain and dropped to the ground in a thunderous crash.

"NOOOOOO!" Alex screamed. "You son of bitch!" She got up and lit her fists. With what strength she had left, she managed to punch Sanah. The two of them continued to exchange blows. Alex screamed and kicked Sanah in the stomach as he bent over. Alex formed a knife and went to thrust it in the back of Sanah's neck. Sanah blocked the attack and formed a small spear and thrusted into Alex's side. Alex had no more to give. She tried to say something, anything, but all that came out was a gargle sound as a river of blood dripped from her mouth. Alex looked Sanah straight into the eye in shock before she looked down at the purple lit sword that was impaled in her side. He pushed it and Alex could feel it breaking free on the other side of her body. She felt the sword leave her body as Sanah pulled it back. She just dropped to the ground. She stared at Komptin's lifeless body before she fell face forward. Sanah managed to roll her over on her back. He stood over her, staring at her. "There is no one to help you now." He formed another bow staff with a sharp end and went to stab her.

Sanah screamed in pain as he looked down at his chest at the glowing red fist sticking out of it. The fist retracted as Sanah tried to breathe as he turned around. The last thing he saw was a red glowing knife thrust into his eye socket as he fell to the ground.

Alex watched Sanah's body fall. It landed next to her with a blank stare. His remaining eye was looking at her while the other was hollowed out. His body disintegrated and Alex looked up to see Roger standing over her. He had grown big since she had last seen him. He had a grin on his face as he held out his hand. "Be mine, you will live, and we will produce something truly amazing," he offered her.

Vandor appeared over Roger's shoulder. He knelt to Alex's ear and whispered, "All you have to do is say 'yes'."

Roger held out his hand with a faint glow of red in his eyes. "Do you accept? What could you possibly have to lose?"

Vandor dug his claws into Alex's side where Sanah had pierced through her body. The burnt skin amplified the pain. Alex could feel that she had no alternative. She knew it was time to accept her fate. Alex tried to talk but could not get it out.

Vandor leaned in, "What is that, my dear? What could you lose?"

"My faith," Alex was able to get out. "When you look to the stars, you think of this moment, okay? You black, soulless, piece of sh..."

Vandor's face drew angry as he picked up her head and smashed her against the ground. "She isn't going to cave. We'll have to go with Plan 4."

"And what about her?" Roger asked Vandor as he stared at her.

"Leave her to die, alone, knowing she's a failure," Vandor said.

Roger looked down at her, "Too bad, Alex, you don't know what you could have had." He cleared his throat and spat on Alex. "She's always been a royal bitch anyways," he said, walking away with Vandor.

All Alex heard next was the sound of Komptin dragging himself over to Alex and curling up next to her. The two of them laid there as the darkness started to overcome their Lite.

Chapter 13

The sound of someone walking was all that could be heard in this sea of death. Ariel and Devine walked ahead of Celestial, overseeing the bodies lying on the ground. "It appears we are too late," Ariel said as she turned over one of the empty shells of a young man. Ariel tried to hide the mangled body from Celestial to see.

"We should find her body," Devine pointed out. She walked ahead a bit, scouting over the bodies which laid lifeless.

Celestial looked to her two guardians, "Oh, why is that?"

"She deserves a proper burial," they both said under their breaths. They scanned the remnants of the bodies that the infiltrators had torn apart. They were hoping to find clues as to where Alex's remains were. The two of them gave each a look of fear as if there was no hope of finding any sign of her.

They continued to walk around the empty bodies that once encased the lives of these young influential people. Celestial was becoming overburdened with grief as she came across each of the pointless deaths of the young humans. She saw the body of a young man who could not have been more than sixteen years of age. She knelt next to him and grabbed his hand. The young boy was shivering, scared. Celestial grabbed a jacket and folded it so the boy's head was resting on it. The boy looked at Celestial with his quivering lip.

"It's cold," the boy admitted as his body shook. He had been torn open by infiltrators.

"Shhh," Celestial said softly as she looked over the wounds of the boy. She put her hand on his forehead.

"I'm so scared," he started crying. "I don't want to die."

Celestial held back her tears. "All He asks of you is to believe," she told him in a soft voice.

"I don't deserve forgiveness," the boy pleaded. Tears rolled down his face, "It hurts so much."

Celestial gave him a caring smile and put her hand on the boy's chest. "What does your heart tell you?" A light came underneath her hand as the boy grasped his last breath. Celestial put her hand on the young boy's forehead and recited a small forgiveness prayer. She took a moment before she stood up to see Ariel and Devine standing still, staring down at a body. Celestial slowly approached the two angels.

"Ariel, Devine," Celestial softly said in a calming but worried voice as she came up behind the two of them. Devine was leaning on her bow staff as support and Ariel looked away up to the sky. Celestial put her hand on Devine's shoulders as she pulled herself in between them. Celestial looked down at the lifeless body of Alexandria who was lying in mud that was made up of dirt and blood. Komptin was next to her, lying still in his gargoyle state in a protective position. "It seems he kept his promise to Osiah; to protect her until his last breath." Celestial bent down to pull the hair from Alex's face.

"She was so strong," Devine said.

"She deserves to be a star of Heaven," Ariel pointed out.

Celestial looked up to her guardians as she could see the both of them were showing signs of sorrow. Celestial had known the two of them since first light and could never remember them shaking up over a human's death before. The faint sounds of sirens were heard coming in the distance. "We should get Komptin out of here before he is seen in his gargoyle state."

Ariel and Devine bent over to pick up Komptin, "Man, he is heavy," they said. It took the two of them to carry the body of Komptin towards the door. They made it a couple of feet before Devine stopped and looked down at Komptin. She had to make sure as she held the massive head of Alex's protector. "Mistress," Devine called for her.

Ariel followed up, "Ah, Madam,"

Celestial got up and came up to them. Celestial looked down at the faint glow of blue light emanating from Komptin's eyes. There was not much there but hopefully enough. "Komptin," Celestial said. "Stay, do not go," she kissed him, placing her hand on his forehead. He started to shake and then broke free from the Guardian's grasp. He crashed to the ground and howled in pain.

He crawled to Alex's body using only his front legs. He refused to leave her side. "Komptin," Celestial said. All she saw was the refusal to leave Alex behind.

"If we take her body, her family and friends will live their lives on this planet in constant grief; they will receive no closure," Celestial pointed.

262

"Would you want to do that to Kale and Anne?" Komptin nudged Alex with his massive head, hoping for some sign of life in her. He gave a painful howl of sadness when the three angels put their caring hands on his torn body. He hesitantly tried to walk on all fours, blue blood from his chest was spilling onto the ground. Ariel and Devine did not hesitate to help him.

Komptin refused their help. "There is nothing wrong with receiving help," Devine told him.

"Even the strongest warrior needs someone to lean on from time to time," Ariel pointed out. Komptin morphed into his dog state in agonizing pain. Ariel ripped a piece of her clothes and placed it on his chest. Ariel held it with her hand as she picked up Komptin and headed towards the door.

"She does not deserve to be found alone," Devine stated.

"The people's authorities will be here soon," Ariel commented.

Celestial looked around, "Clean her up the best you can before their police and rescue personnel arrive."

Devine nodded in agreement as she bent over to move the body. A small wince from Alex's face caught her attention. "ALEX!" Devine yelled. Celestial went running to the body which Devine was holding.

"Alexandria, my dear," Celestial said. "If you are still with us, do not go." She stroked her hand back into her hair. "I promise you, if you do not give up, you will find what you are looking for."

Alex slowly moved her head. Devine quickly ran over to place her down on the ground. She ripped off the sash she had around her waist and covered Alex with it. "Komptin," Alex tried to speak. The sound of a growl caught Celestial and Devine's attention.

"We do not have time for this," Devine formed her bow staff. She instantly turned to pierce the head of an infiltrator as it howled in pain as it diminished. "There may be more," Devine told Celestial.

"I will help Ariel with Komptin. Alexandria needs to get to a hospital, get her there. Protect her." Celestial asked as she got up.

"As if she was you," Devine promised.

Celestial joined Ariel who was close to the door. The two of them vanished into night darkness.

Devine could see the lights coming in the darkness. The flashing red and blue combined with the sound of the sirens meant the human medics and authorities were on their way. Devine took one more look around. She did not hesitate to think of the repercussions as she expanded her misty wings. She quickly but gently grabbed Alex in her arms and took to the sky, carrying her to the hospital.

Once arrived, she quickly diminished her wings and halo. Her body armor disappeared as human outfit emerged. She found the best time to come out of the shadows to carry Alex to the hospital.

"Help!" Devine's voice echoed in the hospital. A group of medical staff rushed over to her.

"What happened to her?" one of the female medics asked.

"I found her lying on the ground like this," Devine said. She gently placed her on the table with wheels as they rolled her off. Devine put her hands on Alex's forehead in a caring fashion before she was carted off.

"I've never seen wounds like this, it looks like burns but the cut was with a knife," the medic said. "Bring her straight to OR." The medic turned around to ask Devine more questions, but she disappeared to join Ariel and Celestial.

***

"She almost died," Father Tom told the Cardinal as they stood outside Alex's hospital room. He shook his head in disbelief. "How'd she do it?"

The Cardinal replied in a calming voice, "She survived because she kept her faith, Father." He was trying to keep quiet as he escorted Father Tom to the waiting area so Alex wouldn't hear. "Our little girl over there is one tough cookie." The Cardinal closed his eyes before reaching the window, looking out over the town's lights. "This organization, it scares me. Man is losing its belief in God. We are in trying times, Father."

Father Tom joined him by his side. "Her friend, Anne has potential to become one of our top historians, but she still isn't a priest or even Catholic."

"Those are just titles," the Cardinal told him. "It matters what is in a person's heart and faith." He turned to look down the hospital hallway. "Father, the Council wants Alexandria to be relocated to D.C. at our church. Create a position in the church for her, something that won't raise too much suspicion."

Father Tom nodded, "And what of Ms. McClure?" he asked as he started writing in his notes.

"Open up a position for her at our church as well," the Cardinal stated. "She can do it from there."

"Yes Cardinal," Father Tom commented.

"The Dark will no doubt start their offense in D.C. They will try to influence community leaders," the Cardinal told him. "She will be in many interactions with her hunts."

"She will spill a lot of blood," Father Tom reminded him.

"Yes," The Cardinal said. "So young," he shook his head. "Her worries should not be fighting the evil of the Dark. We ask so much of her."

"The wounds she will endure will be plenty, she has no one to look after her," Father Tom told him. "What do you suggest we do?"

The Cardinal answered, "We can convert the bottom floor office into a bedroom for her in the rectory. There is a janitor closet next to that office. See if they can connect that to that room to create a private bathroom for her." The Cardinal stared back at the window, "We can be her support; we can be her family."

"I'll get it done," Father Tom stated.

***

Warcourt sat in the F.O.R.'s main meeting place. He knew things did not go as planned but he knew that Vandor and Gron had an alternate plan. They briefed him on what he needed to do. He sat

266

there waiting. He viewed the scratches on his arm from the massive creature and the bruise on his chest from the Lite Sentry. He found a magazine of celebrity gossip that he caught himself reading as a group of the F.O.R. started trickling in.

"What are you doing here?" one of them asked. "What the hell was all of that?"

"Yeah, who was that girl and that thing that interrupted our goal of absolute power?" another had asked.

Warcourt put down his magazine. "So, you are telling me you still accept absolute power?"

"If you could survive the attack from that girl and creature; then yes, that is the type of power we want," the girl pulled out in front said.

"How many are there?"

"Sixteen," the girl answered.

Warcourt got up and looked at the crowd. "Do you still accept my offer of absolute power?"

All of them dropped to their knees as they extended their arms. The group of infiltrators came in behind them and sniffed at their perspective hosts.

"I only need sixteen," Warcourt told the infiltrators with a grin on his face.

***

Alex was in the hospital room, staring out the window in a cold dead stare. The Cardinal and Father Tom had just left. They informed her of the plan to move her to D.C. She was cold, alone, and the fact they would take her in was a sense of security to her. She had the window open for a bit of fresh air when she caught a sense in the air. She overlooked the horizon, as she knew it was a strong sense of Infiltration that had just taken place. She closed the window to see the reflection in the glass and showed her the wound on her face. She lightly touched it when she heard the nurse coming into the room.

"Feeling better?" the nice nurse asked. "You shouldn't be out of bed so soon."

All Alex could do was force a small smile. "I'm not a big fan of beds."

"Well, you have to get some sleep," the nurse said as she refilled the water bottle.

Alex laughed, "Sleep, that's cute."

"Are you okay, dear?" the nurse asked while coming over to her. She saw Alex start to cry. The nurse gently hugged Alex, trying to make sure not to hurt her wounds.

Alex wiped a tear from her face as she returned the hug. "It will sound silly."

"Try me," she said, letting go of Alex.

"I miss my dog," Alex cried. "I lost my best friend."

"Oh, honey, you can get a new dog," the nurse told her, giving her a loving smile.

Alex gazed at the stars trying to figure out which one Komptin was, "Not like that one."

The nurse fixed up the bed for her to get into. "It's getting late, why don't you get into bed."

"In a bit," Alex said. She just stared out the window. Flashbacks of her getting stabbed by Sanah were replaced with a vision of Roger piercing his fist through the chest of Sanah kept on racing through her mind. His hand out asking to join him with the Dark or die in the mud also kept on coming back to her. She put her hand on the window to regain her balance as her phone rang. She answered it, "Hello?"

"Alex? Are you okay," Anne said. "Kale just told me what had happened, he said that you got mugged?"

"That is what I told him," Alex replied.

"I'm going to try to get home as soon as I can," Anne said. "Kale said that he was getting on a flight first thing in the morning."

That made Alex smile hearing that her two friends would drop everything for her. "Anne, I need you to stay there. I need you to learn all that you can if we are going to be in this fight. I have a feeling something big is coming."

"Just as long as you promise to do what the doctors say," Anne said. "Take care of yourself. Love you."

"Love you too," Alex said. "I'll talk to you tomorrow. Bye."

Alex hung up the phone and checked her messages. For some reason she was hoping to hear from the Council.

"You are not as alone as you think you are."

Alex turned around to see Celestial in the doorway. Alex limped over to her as fast as she could and gave her a big hug. "Oh, God, how I wanted to see you."

Celestial returned the hug. "I am glad you are feeling better."

"I...I...I thought I was dead," Alex said.

Celestial looked to the stars, "The thought crossed our minds as well." Celestial walked Alex to her bed. "Come now, child, you need to rest."

"The last thing I remembered was something about finding something," Alex told her as she was getting situated into her bed.

Celestial smiled, "You need to rest."

"I'm actually a little hungry," Alex told her.

Ariel and Devine walked into the room. "Deep fried Oreo?" Ariel asked her as she handed her a bag.

Alex laughed, but winced in pain as she did. "What really sounds good is…"

"Apollo?" Devine held out her hand.

"Thank you," Alex said to the two of them.

Ariel and Devine were on both sides of the bed, "We are going to drop our wings," Devine said.

"If you bring this up again, we will make you pay," Ariel said.

"Bring what up?" Alex asked them.

The two of them at the same time hugged Alex tightly. Ariel was the first to speak, "Fear is something we do not experience often…"

"…and we do not like it," Devine continued.

They stood up and looked down to her, "Do not scare us like that again." They turned around and stood by the window, looking outwards as if they were on the lookout for danger. Alex watched them as they both wiped tears from their face.

"Are they…"

"I would not point that out," Celestial started to tuck Alex into bed.

"Can I ask you something?" Alex asked Celestial as she was getting comfortable.

"Anything," Celestial made sure Alex was snug in bed.

"Can you...can you show me the star where Komptin is?" Alex could feel her stomach turn into knots over the pain of missing her friend. "It would really make me feel better."

"Of course, my child. Close your eyes," Celestial asked her. Alex closed her eyes and felt Celestial touch her forehead. She was whispering something that Alex couldn't make out. "Open your eyes."

Alex opened her eyes to see a big German Shepherd looking at her at the foot of the bed, "Komptin!" She screamed. Komptin's eyes flashed neon blue as he jumped onto the bed and licked her.

"What is that dog doing on her bed?" the nurse came in.

"What dog?" Celestial asked the nurse.

"I thought I saw a dog, weird," the nurse said. "Visiting hours are ending in thirty minutes, please start to say your good-byes."

Alex said, "I'd hate to see you go,"

"We will be around," Celestial said. Komptin got off the bed. "Komptin will be waiting for you to hunt again." Celestial smiled at Alex.

Alex studied Celestial as she smiled at Alex. "Are you going to tell me what I'm looking for?"

Celestial folded Alex's hands on top of her chest, "Honey, you look tired."

Alex felt something she hadn't felt in over four years. She yawned, "Maybe just a couple of minutes." Her eyelids shut and she drifted off to sleep.

Celestial along with Ariel and Devine met on the roof of the hospital. Komptin joined them. The four of them overlooked the town. There were rumblings in the distance.

"The Dark is growing," Devine stated.

"The balance is shifting," Ariel pointed out as they heard a gunshot and a scream.

"Mankind has a lot to learn," Celestial said. "He knows this."

Ariel made the comment, "Mankind does not deserve the sacrifice she offers."

"She needs to be happy as well," Devine added. She continued to look forward but moving her eyes to see Celestial's reaction.

Celestial snickered at them, "Nice try, but I am not going to tell you either."

"What?" they both tried playing it off.

Celestial winked at them. "Let us go home."

They nodded.

Celestial bent over to say good-bye to Komptin. "See you around," she kissed him on the forehead before leaving for the doorway.

"Protect her," Devine said. Komptin's eyes flashed blue.

Ariel looked at the purple star, "She is a good kid. You did a good job." She winked at the purple star as she petted Komptin good-bye.

Komptin stayed behind and patrolled the rooftop of the hospital, ensuring Alex's recovery was not disturbed.

END OF PART II